SWEET & SOUR

by

Dick Wild

Grosvenor House
Publishing Limited

This book is published by
Grosvenor House Publishing Ltd
28-30 High Street, Guildford, Surrey, GU1 3EL.
www.grosvenorhousepublishing.co.uk

A CIP record for this book
is available from the British Library

ISBN 978-1-908596-68-0

Contents

Foreword

A second collection of short, simple (sometimes not so sweet) tales drawn from a range of situations, encompassing a range of styles. Aimed at anyone with an eye for a simple stark tale and without the need to be too uplifted by the things they read.

An Evening With
the Camera Club

The camera club was well established, but like a number of its fellow societies up and down the country, a little frayed around the edges in these bleak days of 'snap-shot' imagery and digital gimmickry that accompanied it. Few people it seemed, still had the passion that a number of years ago would have been commonplace the length and breadth of the land. These days, poking your mobile phone in the air for a millisecond was as far as many people's photographic energies were inclined to stretch – particularly the younger people – or so it seemed.

But the spirit was still there in a number of old die-hards and the club limped along with its time and tested calendar of monthly competitions, guest speakers and occasional excursions to churches, river estuaries, autumnal woods and flower shows.

It was a predominantly 'male' affair – and 'elderly male' at that, but they were a hard-core of devotees and still willing to 'fight for the cause' - in the wake of the digital revolution - and at each and every club evening, spirited conversations on the latest lenses, old Rolleiflexes, snags with 'autofocus' and the ins and outs of 'depth of field' preview buttons were testament to their unflinching passion. That very evening, Greg and Roy, two of the longest standing members were absorbed in conversation trying to recall whether the old SLR Minolta SR7 was the first with a built in CDS meter. Neither was sure, though they *had* been certain that the lens flange fitting *was* in fact a triple bayonet clutch.

On this particular evening a guest 'expert' had been booked to give an appraisal of some current prints by a handful of photographers, who'd been working mostly abroad in some of the world's most war-torn areas, and had now returned to the UK. to promote a book. Prints from the book had been released in advance to certain affiliated bodies as part of a promotion, following a recent slump in the retail sales of photographic books, though the prints were not yet available on general release.

Upon receipt of the prints, the club had decided it might be nice to make an evening of it and put the prints on view to their members, under the adjudicative eye of a local 'judge'

The 'judge' in question was a 'competition judge' of considerable local renown. And though not a local herself – residing as she did in a little village some way out in a rural part of Essex – she had often been prepared to pop down to the club to judge their monthly competitions and the club members had invariably found her comments and evaluations to be both instructive and informative. She had accordingly been invited to offer her appraisal of the prints at tonight's session and had gratefully accepted the invitation.

As ever, she'd arrived appropriately dressed, for it was after all a formal event in the club's diary and the members who paid her fee would expect her to make an effort and present herself accordingly. For this evening's engagement she had opted for a sharp three-quarter length skirt, puffed sleeve blouse necktie and smart navy jacket. She smiled warmly at the assembled as she took her place at the front of the hall, to be introduced by the club secretary Bill. After receiving a warm welcome and expressing her thanks for the invitation, she began proceedings. She was exceptionally 'well-spoken', having acquired an almost 'received-pronunciation' accent as befits one who has nudged her way into middle age in one of Essex's particularly pleasant and most sought-after rural villages.

She began the evening's proceedings by pointing out that she was of course simply offering a *personal* response to these prints and that there could be no *absolute* in undertaking analyses of other photographers' work. She'd gathered that many, if not all of the pictures on view tonight were from foreign parts, which would be interesting, and add a sense of 'adventure' to the evening. She also pointed out that her personal area of 'work' was 'floral still-life' and 'cats'; but it must be remembered that there's always something to be gained from observations beyond ones' customary genres.

With that she turned momentarily, as the first print was taken from its protective shield and placed on the purpose-built easel with specially designed fluorescent illumination built in at the top.

'Well now, what have we here to get our evening underway?' she asked, taking a pause to eye the 'work' and clasp her hands together in consideration.

'Clearly a piece from foreign parts. We can deduce as much from the setting with its shacks and people occupying the bulk of the foreground. It's in fact, a lively little street scene – little flurries of activity evenly spaced in the composition and these rather homespun little shacks that the people appear to live in. Our eye is of course immediately drawn into the left side of the print, where the woman very cleverly manages to carry her wares on her head and this of course creates a sense of movement toward the centre of the frame. We have one or two focal points on the right, but a little uninteresting it has to be said – a pile of baskets and a broken shack entrance not being ideal subjects and ideally we need a little more there – perhaps a snake poking its little head out of the basket or maybe a rather forlorn child standing in the doorway on the right. There is also considerable loss of detail in this whole foreground area (points to area on print) which perhaps could have been retained or emphasised using filters during the printing stage, and there's a little more work to be done in this respect. In summation I'd say a six, or seven out of ten for our author's efforts in this opening print.'

The assistant waited until she signalled that she had said everything that there was to be said on the piece and then took it from the easel and replaced it with the second print. There was a moment's pause as the expert collected her thoughts on the new picture placed before her.

'So…still evidently in a foreign land, judging from the woman there on the left and the fact that it features soldiers on duty which one wouldn't expect in the UK.'

She took another pause for the thoughts middling around in her head to take some semblance of order.

'Interesting overall construction of the image. Notice how we have the soldier on the right – the one in tears – placed in that lower third area, which provides a nice balance. And…. we can see the face! She made the point emphatically, turning to face the members by way of emphasis.

'However, I must say that it would benefit from an added point of interest somewhere up here on the left; maybe a small cat curled in a small recess in the wall, or maybe a local peering out of the window waving to the soldiers. But….its an interesting idea and overall I'd say that the piece works quite well.'

She stopped and took a step back for a final observation and for the assistant - club treasurer - to withdraw the print, place it nearby on a mat and replace it with the next. Together, the club members and the expert gave the third print a few seconds quick perusal, before she continued.

'Well, we're still in foreign climes – the same author, one assumes – and again we have our key point of interest suitably placed here (points) in the lower region of the composition. In this case a wagon loaded with what appears to be bodies; although it is possible of course that they could be taking an afternoon siesta – as is the custom in many of these parts – but then one wonders why in the back of a wagon and why some of them are in effect lying across each other. I'd be more inclined to presume that they are dead – which of course adds interest and creates a story element to the composition. It's a little unfortunate that the author didn't close up a little on their faces to catch their expressions and I'd suggest that the shot would have benefited from the use of a longer lens. However, there are merits in the 'work' and I would commend the author for his choice of an interesting subject and dealing with it as effectively as he could in what, after all, might have been less than ideal circumstances. We move on...'

As the picture was about to be replaced, a hand went up – it was Gordon – a lifelong devotee of the club and something of an expert in autumnal leaves and fauna. He leant forwards looking a little awkward.

'Could I just make a comment?' he asked.

'Of course, feel free....There's no reason why we can't share ideas – one of the beauties of photography is that we all bring a personal perspective to the art, which could - and should – be shared.....pray speak....'

'Well I agree with you that the men in the wagon are more than likely dead and of course with them being positioned very much on the right, it would be nice if there was something on the left to restore some sense of balance – and if there was someone perhaps pointing a rifle out of one of those windows on the left, it would be like he'd shot them and that would add another idea and create a little more interest in the picture.'

'Yes...I take your point,' she said, 'there is a sort of uneasy feeling about the print at the moment, which is, as you rightly point out is to do with a sense of imbalance – there's a lifeless quality to the overall composition which tends to leave us with a feeling of dissatisfaction.....But we move on...Next please.'

The next photograph was carefully placed on its easel and the customary few moments taken for all to observe.

'This is an interesting picture isn't it – the mother cradling her baby gently in her arms. One wonders whether the baby is sleeping or, like our friends in the last work – dead. My suspicions are that the child is dead – note the expression on the mother's face as she gently holds her young baby. The light isn't of course ideal here and we have some difficulty in making out her features. Perhaps it would have been more successful to return later in the day – or of course earlier – depending on which would provide a better angle of light. 'Earlier' may not have been an option of course, as the child might have been alive at that point.

One feature definitely worthy of note here – and I do hope you spotted it – is the tremendous sky. Note the 'burning-in' on these clouds rendering them a brooding, almost threatening quality that works exceptionally well. However, returning to the lower part of the frame, I'd have liked to see a bit more in the mother's face – maybe a few tears trickling gently down her cheeks – One almost feels inclined to point out to her that her child is dead, just in case it hasn't quite registered, but as we said earlier, it isn't always easy to get the 'ideal' picture in such circumstances and perhaps we have to make some concessions in some respects......So we move on...'

Her assistant launched into his familiar manoeuvre to withdraw the print from the easel and replace it with the final print of this particular photographer.

Again there was a moment's pause as the expert took a step back to gauge an overall perspective of the 'work', before offering her critique.

'Well, our friend certainly succeeded in capturing the mood of the scene in this one, showing an excellent sense of timing – being ready and waiting just at the moment when the rather unfortunate man's leg is being blown off – we see the limb still passing through the air here in the upper foreground – caught superbly by the deployment of a fast shutter speed. Of course there's a fair gushing of blood to add to the urgency and sense of drama. But again it has to be said that there's something of an imbalance – with all the action, as it were, placed in the lower right third area. Ideally we need something of comparable eye-catching attraction happening over here (points to left of print) – a second limb caught in mid air perhaps, or maybe a body writhing in its last agonies, or even a cat curled fast asleep against the wall here at the side; just something to provide that balance and improve the overall composition. Still, as we have said 'candid shots' such as this, can be quite difficult to get and under the circumstances our author has chosen an interesting idea which mostly succeeds in engaging our attention....And that I think concludes the work from our first photographer.

So what do we say to the author as a summative appraisal of what we have seen thus far? Certainly he's chosen some interesting subjects and has succeeded in engaging our attention for the most part. There are some flaws in the works which could be addressed and overall I'm going to award the prints six and a half out of ten....And so we move on.....'

And move on they did. Three further collections of prints from some of the world's most torn and troubled zones were unveiled - and placed upon the easel before their eyes for their perusal and inspection.

There were a number of strengths to be observed in the work; and there were flaws of course – not surprisingly so – but the point of course is to 'learn'....and as proceedings drew to a close, the expert turned and with a smile stood to face her audience..

'And let that be the message from the evening; that we learn; and we learn together – and in so doing, we all of us gain just a little and thus take our photography a few steps further forwards.'

There was a pause and a round of applause. A vote of thanks followed from the club secretary, who pointed out that her comments – as ever - had been both instructive and thought-provoking and he was sure that as she'd suggested, they'd all gained something as a result.

She acknowledged the compliment and left the room to a further round of applause and her car parked just around the corner of the building. As she purred her way off up the road, she reflected on what had been a pleasant evening. She certainly enjoyed popping off to various clubs to give them the benefit of her expertise, but she had to admit that she also looked forward to returning to her little cottage and was thankful that for the next few days she had no commitments, affording her the time to potter about in her little garden amongst the roses and chrysanthemums – and maybe take a picture or two – who knows... She moved on.

Crime of Passion

There was once a couple who didn't get on too well and seemed to spend all their time rowing like cat and dog. So one day, in an apparent attempt to 'clear the air' they took a stroll in the countryside, ostensibly hoping that a few hours in rural surroundings might calm their minds and enable them to see each other in a more favourable light.

Both were both youngish to middle-aged, maybe early thirties; she – a rotund woman with stocky bull-like legs, whilst he was a gangly-built man with a Rasputin-type shock of hair and long looping arms that dangled and flopped down his sides like an ape's.

The grass was long in the field that they had found themselves in – at times almost waist height. The woman led the way, scrabbling through the long reedy undergrowth, almost struggling to keep her balance, followed by her husband, also stumbling along, his tentacle-like arms sweeping the air in an attempt to maintain forward momentum.

Occasionally, she stopped and looked back, calling after him in short cat-call bursts of irritation, until, reminding herself that, to all intents and purposes, they were attempting to lighten their differences rather than exacerbate them, she relented and waited for him to draw level, rebuking him only mildly for being so slow. He pointed out that it wasn't his fault: the grass was so long, walking through it was difficult. She pointed out that she had managed to keep ahead by some distance. But to avoid things escalating to yet another row, she changed the subject, suggesting they take a seat and set about eating their picnic. He concurred and they flopped down, nestling themselves into a comfortable position.

They had imagined they were alone in the field, for there had been no signs of life since they had left the country lane. But, unbeknown to them, a man was perched some seventy yards above, the long unkempt grass effectively shielding him from vision. His name was John – a quiet bespectacled man with a jovial easy-going nature. He had watched the pair's approach with a tinge of regret, for he had taken his break in the countryside to get away from it all for a while, to relax and read his book in a little solitude.

He watched the couple settle into place, a little dismayed that they had chosen to park themselves so close, but he had developed a liking for this particular spot near the brow of the hill with the fence on the left and a small thicket of trees down round the stream below. And were he to 'up himself' and make a move, he would draw attention, which was something he preferred not to do.

So he resolved to stay put, mind his own business and read his book. He re-set himself comfortably in the grass and returned his eyes to the page.

Beneath him, the couple's enmity was showing signs of resurgence. The husband was spilling clumps of blueberry muffin in the grass under the watchful eye of his wife who was becoming increasingly irritated.

'You're dropping most of it,' she said.

'The moles can 'ave it,' he replied.

'Can't even eat a muffin.'

'Shut up. It's only a muffin.'

He looked her in the face, his resentment expressed in exaggerated movements of his lower jaw. But nothing more was said and she turned her attention to a second Tupperware box containing packets of cheese and onion crisps and two Yorkie bars.

Her husband watched her fumbling attempts to release the lid and then – grinning impishly – he leant forwards aiming a playful punch at her arm.

She told him to stop, her irritation undiminished from earlier.
He appeared not to hear, continuing to grin and paw at her at arm's length.
She rebuked him further, her voice levelled more pointedly in his direction.
The punches were actually a gesture of endearment rather than provocation, prompted by sexual arousal which had been stirring from the moment he'd stepped over the gate and first entered the field.
He had been a lifelong devotee of 'sex in the outdoors' (albeit at a purely academic level) since his schooldays, when, one lunch-time round the back of the bike-sheds, some older boys had allowed him a quick shufti at their 'Health And Efficiency' magazines.

His wife, who shared no such inclinations, and was by far the more level-headed of the two, was nonetheless aware of his game and quickly turned on him – his predisposition to indecency being another of the things that irritated her about him. Unfortunately her husband, being of weak resolve, invariably found attempts to deflect his attentions giving rise to bouts of irritation and aggression. He continued to paw her and give her the seductive eye, suggesting that they forget the crisps and get down into the long grass.

But she was having none of it and rebuked him further, sitting up and brushing her hands – a clear signal for him to put an end to his shenanigans. He tried bringing his hand in contact with her lower back, venturing under her shirt and rotating his finger against the bare flesh, but to no avail. She drew herself free and shifted a few feet to her left, re-positioning herself at a secure distance.
As she settled into place and looked across, the leering expression on his weasely face almost made her gag and brought home to her just how repugnant he was and how much she despised him.

She finally succeeded in removing the lid from the Tupperware box and placed it on the grass.

Conceding defeat he sulkily withdrew his arm and told her she was an uptight fucked-up bitch. She began to peel the wrapper off one of the Yorkie bars and told him he was a sad deranged little pervert.

John turned a custard cream in his fingers and took a nibble. A slight breeze had drifted from the copse to his right and there was a distinct darkening in the sky to the west. He was within earshot of the couple below, but awarded them little attention. He had his book and later he would go to the pub and drink four and a half pints of ale. He took another bite of the biscuit and turned the page.

The man was telling his wife she was a fucked up tramp but she wasn't listening. She was watching a squirrel scampering its way up the branch of a tree, intrigued by the way it stopped statue-like every three or four feet.

When her husband finished his apple and petulantly flung the core in her direction, narrowly missing her left ear, she simply turned on him and in a controlled and measured voice, told him not to be so childish. That was another thing that annoyed her about him. As well as being pathetic and indecent, he was childish; childish and repulsive.

She returned her attention to the tree, where a second squirrel had appeared and was furtively scurrying back and forth, toward, and then away from, the first squirrel in quick darting movements. She marvelled at the simplicity of it all and would have liked nothing more than to lie back in the grass and feel 'at one' in the whole rich environment, but realised it would be impossible without her husband crawling across and pawing at her like a dog.

But it was later, when she looked over her shoulder to inform him of her up and coming plans, that the real trouble started and any chance of patching up their differences ended.

The light breeze had hardened as John removed the cling-film from his Brie and pickle roll and sank his teeth into the soft squidgy dough. As he chewed and watched the increasingly threatening clouds gathering to his right, he did his best to turn a deaf ear to the recriminations and counter-recriminations, that, by now, resonated like gun-fire across the meadow below.

It was at about five minutes later that matters finally got out of hand.

A particularly vociferous outpouring of scorn was followed by what appeared to be frantic rustlings in the grass.

Moments later, the air, the sky, the whole valley it seemed, was shattered as two gunshots ricocheted across the field, involuntarily flattening John into the grass, freezing him into horizontal recline.

For what felt like an eternity, he lay still, cannonballs bouncing in his chest, wondering what the fuck was going on. And it was some time before he had gathered himself sufficiently to peer down in the direction from whence the gunshots had come.

The scene was, for once, shrouded in silence. He could see the man sitting, staring down at the body at his side. He appeared to be holding a gun in his right hand.

John, quick to resume his horizontal position, was busily contemplating his next move, which, for the time being at least, involved little beyond staring at the sky with an overriding sense of foreboding.

Below him the man was also in a state of shock. Since shooting his wife, he had remained seated in the grass, his stare alternating between the gun hanging in his right hand and the limp body at his side.

It was only when raw panic kicked in, that – on looking round – he noticed a figure or what appeared to be a figure, partly hidden amongst the clumps of grass some sixty or seventy yards above him. He gave it a good long stare, as if to confirm that it *was* a person and not just a tree stump or a plastic bundle left lying in the grass. And then, after brief consideration and with gun in hand, he made his move.

John was telling himself, or trying to tell himself, to stay calm. He had toyed with making a run for it across the field, but realised that could make him an ideal second target. His best move was to do nothing, to stay put; this was nothing to do with him. He was simply minding his own business, having a quiet afternoon in the countryside.

He was still convincing himself of such when he saw the figure bounding up the slope towards him.

At a distance of about ten yards the figure stopped, fixing his eyes on John as might a jungle creature scrutinizing an unwanted scavenger on its territory. The man's appearance: exploding hair and dangling ape-like arms confirmed the need to remain calm and keep things, or try to keep things, on a level.

The man had the gun held firmly in his right hand and was clearly in a state of some confusion. He switched his eyes from John to the bottom of the slope, prompting John to follow suit. He looked back and for the first time, spoke.

'See what I done?' he said, flicking his head, gesturing down toward the lower side of the grassy slope.

John promptly shook his head, lips drawn.

'I shot my wife,' the man explained, still glancing down the hill, checking for any sign of movement. He turned again.

'I shot her twice.'

John – content to do the listening, and, for the time being, at least, have the man keep on talking – had his eye fixed on the gun.

'But she had it coming,' he said.

'Do you understand what I'm saying?' He looked away. 'She definitely had it coming. Crime of passion. That's what it is.'

John nodded, his eye still on the gun hanging loosely from the dishevelled arm. The man raised the arm and peered vacantly at the short barrel – the immediate source of his problem.

'She was playing away, you see.' he said. 'Stupid thing is....she don't even like sex – and then only missionary...It don't make sense.'

He turned his eyes towards the brow of the hill.

'But she wouldn't listen – never did. I warned her I'd blow her brains out. She just laughed, so I blew her brains out. She didn't know I had a gun. But I did. Thought I might bag a few rabbits. Bloke she was seeing empties the bins down the care-home.'

He turned to John and as a warning gesture, shook the gun a few times in his hand.

'You see what I'm saying.'

John nodded.

For all his dishevelled appearance, the man appeared to have had a clear enough grasp of his predicament. As if to prove the point, he looked up.

'But we have a problem,' he said, waving the gun again in John's direction. 'Problem is...you've seen everything. You watched what happened. You have a description. You can go from here, give the police their description and have me sent down. What's your name?'

'John.'

'I'm Eddie.'

'Hi Eddie.'

Eddie looked down.

'You're safe for the moment,' he said. 'But you understand. You can have me sent down.' There was a moment for John to consider his position – *both* their positions.

'But.... I'm going to need your help,' he added, looking back and toting the gun warningly in the air.

'We got to move quickly,' he said. 'It's quiet for the moment, but you can never tell what's going to happen. I got to get her off the scene before anyone sees her......Come on.'

He flicked the gun as indication for the pair of them to make a move. 'I'm going to need your help.' He was glancing anxiously across the fields and thickets as he spoke.

John knew the need to play it cool. Whatever he intended, he would go along with, whatever he requested, he would, at least for the moment, agree to.

15

He rose and at the invitation of Eddie's gun, picked up his shoulder bag and began the stroll down the hill, closely followed by Eddie, whose eye strayed repeatedly back and forth across the surrounding fields.

'Stupid fucking woman,' he said, half stumbling on the plodding tufts and clumps of grass under his feet. 'It didn't have to be like this.' His left arm hovered slightly to help him maintain his balance. 'Didn't have any brains, that was her trouble. Never did.'

On reaching the spot, Eddie broke to his right, circumnavigating the scene, leaving John with the crumpled body lying in the grass; the head resting on the arm as if in the midst of a late afternoon nap, the right leg twisted under the left. A pool of crimson had soiled her blouse and had spread over much of her head. Eddie returned and looked down and then flicked his head in the direction of the wooded thicket down in the stream valley just below.

'Got to get her down there – down into the trees,' he said, already breathless from his exertions.

'What you going to do with her?' asked John, seeing a little two-way communication as maybe a way of easing both their situations. Eddie nodded in the direction of the thicket and indicated the area with a flick of his gun.

'There's a pipe,' he said. 'One of them big round grey stone pipes down there by the stream, hidden behind the trees. We've got to get her down there – and stick her in it.'

He wiped his brow and twitched the gun a few more times. John looked down at the area indicated. There was little to be seen behind the mass of foliage and branches whirling and swaying in the breeze.

Eddie's mind was racing, his eye caught between his plan-of-action waiting for him down in the thicket and his wife lying limp and bloodied in the grass beneath him. John too was doing his share of thinking whilst trying to avert his eyes from the dead woman. He had rarely seen dead people and was finding the stillness of it disturbing; he couldn't help thinking she looked like a roll of carpet dumped by a passing car. The crimson had layered a good deal of her face and upper torso and had run into dark bluey purple patches in the surrounding grass.

Eddie had tucked the gun into his waist band and wandered a few feet down towards the bushes and stream where he glanced quickly into the depths of green and then scurried back to the body.

'Pipe's over there,' he said, nodding down in the general direction of the stream. 'We'll get her down there first so she's out of the way.' He stood a moment, taking a final glance at his wife, his eyes fixed on her scarlet covered face.

Then he leant to her feet and made a few initial grabs for her ankles.

'Which end do you want?' he asked.

John looked at the gun hooked down the waistband of Eddie's trousers and had a sudden bizarre vision of the gun firing and his bollocks being shot to pieces. Returning to the question, he looked across, resolved – even at this stage – to try and have him think seriously about what he was proposing. He too looked down towards the thicket.

'She's dead Eddie, she'll be found anyway,' he said, thinking it appropriate enough, given the circumstances, to resort to first name terms.

'Not stuffed in a pipe she won't. Not for a while anyway.'

Eddie had abandoned his wife's ankles and was clearing the area in their immediate vicinity.

'Got to move her,' he said. 'Can't leave her here. She'll be well hidden – there's twigs, all sort of shit to cover her with – she'll be better off there. Can't just leave her lying in a field.'

John looked at Eddie, and at his wife, and sighed.

'I'll take her feet,' he said, arching his way towards Eddie, who nodded and made his way to his right, towards her top end.

'Right – and no funny stuff,' Eddie warned, pausing briefly to tap the gun handle. 'I'm not afraid to use this. I've used it once and I'll use it again.' John nodded and turned his attention to the woman's lower end.

The first problem was manoeuvring her from her lying position. Eddie took a few quick tugs at her arms and then her shoulders to assess the best means of securing a grip, his fingers toiling with the bloodied head and soiled blouse and still grumbling at his third attempt to ease her shoulders clear of a grassy clump.

He stopped, eyeing his stained hands and waiting for John to make some headway with her ankles. He had his back to the uneven surface and her head and shoulders weighed heavily in his arms, one or the other dripping steadily in the waves of grass. He heaved a little harder.

'Reckoned I was perverted,' he said, seeing their opening steps as ideal opportunity to open the case for his defence. 'Not true.' John had a grasp on her lower legs, but kept the pressure of her feet against him to take the pair of them, or three of them, toward a ridge a few feet away.

'Fact is she was fucked up,' Eddie said. 'Fucked up and frigid – didn't even like sex, and then only missionary. And with her fancy bin-emptying prick!'

John was relieved that they had managed to fall into a kind of rhythm, which would at least keep them moving. The wind had strengthened and the swirling tree tops and bushes hinted of oncoming rain.

They staggered a further twenty or so to the beginning of a thicket of trees leading down a sharper incline, where, at a distance of some twenty yards upstream, the pipe could be seen protruding from a break in the earth and tree rooting.

'Good idea. We'll pick them up later,' said Eddie, concurring with John's decision to remove her shoes and let them drop in the grass.

'Her and shoes,' Eddie said, still staggering under her weight. 'Always buying shoes, got hundreds of them. Bottom of our wardrobe's like fucking Auschwitz. Watch you don't slip on this wet bit.'

Care was needed at a point where the surface dipped to its more urgent descent to the stream. Eddie was gasping – exasperated that a human being – particularly his wife – could be so awkward and cumbersome to shift from A to B.

'Looks a mess, don't she?' he said, laying her to the ground, allowing her to flop a little towards the stream. He stood a moment, wiping his brow.

'Used to reckon I was scruffy, used to call me 'Scruffbag' – I used to call her 'porky' on account of her fat legs. She said scruffy looks could be changed. I said 'so can fat legs - go on a diet.' He leant to grab her once more by the arms.

John was gauging the best route to get them nearer the stream. He took a breath and watched Eddie give his dangling limbs a shake before reaching once more for her head.

'Ain't saying much now is she?' Eddie said, poking an exploratory leg toward a twisted oak tree slightly down the banking. 'Makes a change having her around with her gob shut for more than five minutes.'

On a count of three he took hold of her upper torso, waiting for John to find his footing.

'We'll just get down to that little path, then we can get her up to where the stream begins. At least her head's stopped dripping.'

It was a few yards later that they were able to take their next break, seating themselves on tufts of grass close to the stream.

Eddie lit a cigarette.

'Always on about money.' He pocketed the lighter and blew the opening exhalations towards his wife's feet.

'Used to reckon I was lazy. I ain't lazy. It ain't easy getting work these days. I'd tell her but she never listened. *She* was lazy, fucked-up, lazy….and frigid. Couldn't even fry eggs.'

He looked over the stained flesh and flicked the cigarette ash toward the stream. 'Aint easy getting work,' he said. 'Do you work?'

John nodded.

'In a bank,' he said. 'Barclays in town.'

Eddie nodded and stubbed the cigarette before placing it behind the lobe of his ear. He was looking up as he spoke.

'Come on, got to get her in the pipe. Time's getting on.'

They made it another fifteen feet or so to where a protruding tree root that had inconsiderately placed itself in their path. They laid the body and caught their breath.

'Fucking heavy, ain't she?' Eddie puffed his cheeks and wiped a thin residue of blood from his left wrist. He leant against the trunk of the twisted oak tree and stared down, his eyes lingering on the points of her breasts, his finger easing the gun inside the waistband of his trousers.

'Never seen her so quiet,' he said. 'See that top she's wearing, cost about fifty quid – then she says we ain't got no money; talks a load of bollocks.'

John already had his eye on the pipe and the likely mish-mash of refuse waiting for them within it.

Fortunately its opening was somewhere around waist height – serving what purpose, stuck out there half-way along a stream valley, was anybody's guess and was of little concern to Eddie, who scurried a few piles of leaves and twigs from the entrance to peer into its depths.

'We'll get her in there,' he said, an air of confidence growing by the second. 'Just need to clear some of his shit out of the way first.' He moved in to drag a morass of sodden foliage, beer cans, waste paper and fungi-matted clothing into piles and dribs and drabs around their feet.

'Stuff people leave in pipes,' he said, adding a Wellington boot to the heap beneath him.

For a moment John contemplated Eddie's semi-insertion in the pipe as an opportunity to make a break for it, but it demanded a quick decision – too quick on this occasion, and there was always that element of risk, confirmed moments later as Eddie re-appeared from the hole brushing his hands and looking thoughtful. He stood a moment, brushing sweat from his brow, giving the pipe entrance a good hard stare.

'Okay, got to get the pipe cleared first,' he said, his eyes jumping from the piles of rubbish still caked within, to its sisterly pile currently lying in the stream.

He turned to John and with a hand on the gun handle – a reminder that he was, to all effect, still being held at gunpoint – indicated that he should clamber his way into the pipe and draw the remaining rubbish out, whilst Eddie would oversee its descent into an orderly pile on the ground.

He watched as John heaved himself, commando-style, inside the pipe – struggling to avoid contact with its contents until he found himself deep enough to reach most of the remaining mess.

'That's right,' said Eddie, watching him beginning to haul the crap to the end. Fortunately, the months or years of wetness had maintained a lubrication of sorts, between it and the concrete surround, though the odour was unimagineable.

'Good,' said Eddie, seemingly oblivious to the smell and watching as John dumped the shit to the side of the stream at his feet. It took a few more forays, Eddie's hand tightening on the gun handle as John clambered out.

He delved to the bracken and grabbed his wife's shoulders, raising her head to his lap. Together, they staggered her over to the area just in front of the pipe's opening.

'Head first,' said Eddie, bowing slightly to peer into the pipe's recess.

He dumped the head on the grass and made a few further exploratory gauges of the concrete circumference.

'Better get a move on before her rigor-mortis kicks in.' He reached for her arms, taking another perusal across the periphery of trees for any signs of movement.

'That won't happen for a while yet,' said John, clamping his grip on her feet and wishing Eddie would stop dithering. 'Be about another twelve hours before rigor mortis sets in.'

He was still hauling on her legs, attempting to hold her in place and maintain his own equilibrium, as he felt the first drops of rain drifting on the early evening wind and spotting his cheek.

At about the same time, his wife's head started bleeding again, releasing a steady trickle along the nape of her neck to drip into the mud and grass.

'Fuck's sake.' Eddie took a step back and wiped his hands, side-stepping to try and avoid the blood dripping and staining his hands and sleeve any more than it already had. He raised a heel and pressed it against the incline of banking below the lower rim of concrete.

'Need to get her in quick, it's starting to rain; be just like her to get her rigor mortis just as we're stuffing her in the pipe – so we'd have to break her arms and maybe a leg too if it starts poking up in the air.' He turned and leant against the entrance waiting for John to align himself in readiness at the point of entry.

'I threatened to break her legs once when she broke my arm. Dropped a car boot on it while I was fishing her bag out the back. Reckoned it was an accident. I reckon it was deliberate. Told her if she did it again I'd break her legs.'

John was having doubts about her going in head first. It would mean having having the bulk of her to cope with while her feet were still poking out in the air.

'I think she'd be better other way round,' he said, 'Feet first, be easier that way.'

Eddie glanced left to right and then down at his wife, gauging her from tip to toe. 'Okay, you can see better from your angle. We'll do her feet first.'

Together, they rotated the body in a series of short stepping movements like a couple of builders over-laden with bricks.

'Right, feet first, in she goes....That's it.'

Despite the rain and chill Eddie found himself sweating profusely. The enormity of events was beginning to take its toll. The death of his wife was something he'd occasionally mulled over but rarely envisaged tackling from such a close angle as this. The strain was starting to tell.

With her feet inserted, John was able to take the weight of her upper legs to help Eddie push her along. It would prove to be a tight fit, not helped by her body snagging at regular points.

'One two three...push.' They managed about another six inches; she was in up to her waist, but that was all.

Time for another fag break. No need to lay her on the ground now, but the dripping head showed no sign of diminishing and neither Eddie nor John had the means to do much about it. It was simply a question of trying to keep a wide enough berth to keep the blood, or whatever it was, dripping on the floor, away from you. Eddie wiped his forehead leaving a long red streak mingling its way into the matted thatch of hair. 'It was when she told me about this bloke,' he said, bringing the cigarette from his ear to his mouth and reaching for his lighter. 'Bloke who empties the bins down the care-home. That's how she met him. Guy had a job see. Bit of money.' Eddie rubbed his thumb against his fingers. 'Bit of a wanker if you ask me.'

He flicked the ash and looked in John's direction.

'She's sitting there eating a blueberry muffin, and tells me she's making plans – when, fact is – she's already made 'em. What did she expect? Didn't even like sex ....and then only missionary...it don't make sense.'

He turned to John. 'What do you reckon?'

John shrugged.

'It happens Eddie,' he said.

'But it didn't have to. I told her I'd give her another chance but she just laughed. I warned her if she carried on laughing I'd blow her brains out. She carried on laughing so I blew her brains out. She din't know I had a gun. Only brought it to bag a few rabbits.'

Eddie drew on the cigarette and took another look toward the trees at the top of the stream valley, peering through the gaps in the leaves for any sign of movement.

'Come on, we got to get her in,' he said, flicking the fag butt to return to her shoulders.

The pipe's width – or lack of – was a contributory factor. For some minutes they grappled and pulled at her shoulder socket, Eddie wheezing and wriggling her against the concrete perimeter. Finally, with a last ditch shove at a near forty degree angle, they managed to insert her pretty much up to her head. Eddie took a step back and brushed his hands of the smears of blood, contemplating their next move.

'Just give her head another push,' he said, standing back to allow John full access, mindful that without his wife's body between them, he'd be vulnerable to a last ditch assault that might yet see John make his escape into the trees.

John obliged, leaning his full body weight onto his wife's head and squeezing the last few inches of her into, or more or less into, the narrow confines of the pipe.

Eddie stood back and surveyed their work. It was done and a glance along the line of trees confirmed that it had almost certainly been without witnesses.

'Now all we got to do is stuff the crap back,' he said, staring at the piles of refuse and dirt that lay at their feet.

Scoops of black junk, mud and foliage were returned to their home to be stuffed in bits and tiny clumps around her shoulders and smeared liberally around her upper torso and face. Broken twigs and a manky cardigan were draped around her ears and sodden pieces of rotting paper and packaging stuffed against her shoulders and over her head. In the manner of an avant-garde sculptor, Eddie completed the job – cradling layers of mud in his fingers and smearing them liberally over her head until – safely concealed in her pipeline tomb – she was entirely indecipherable as a human being,

As a mark of respect Eddie added a bundle of weeds and a few dandelions and then took a few steps back and brushed his hands, whilst removing the few remaining caches of mud and garbage.

For some time his eyes remained on his wife, trying to come to terms with the fact that the very person who, an hour ago, was berating him for wanting sex in a field, now lay entombed in a waste pipe in the middle of woods. In many respects it just didn't seem to make sense; if she'd used her brains it needn't have come to this.

He turned to John, who had distanced himself in deference to Eddie's final moments with his wife and to take the opportunity to clean himself up as best he could and give some thought to his own immediate future.

He felt reconciled in having done his 'bit' – co-operated with him, humoured him even. He looked at Eddie standing there in the mud – for all his hard-earned efforts – as guilty as the cat with the spilt milk, waiting to be charged with murder.

Eddie turned from the pipe and tapping the gun lightly, signalled for John to lead the way to the top of the ravine back to the field.

For a while the pair stood, like two dishevelled weasels, Eddie's nest of hair reduced to a line of limp strands plastered down his head.

'Stupid woman,' he said, looking back in the direction of the pipe. 'Din't have to be like this.'

He turned to John, his fingers still nursing the gun handle protruding from the waistband of his trousers.

'You done me a favour,' he said, looking down at the gun and slowly withdrawing it, eyeing it ruefully. He looked up.

'I ain't gonna shoot you,' he said. John managed a swift glance at the weapon resting in his palm.

'You going to grass me up?' Eddie asked, looking suddenly anxious, aware perhaps that events were about to drift beyond his control.

John turned to the pipe which – even from where they were standing on the ridge of the ravine – was clearly visible and where, for all their efforts, the clumsy bulge of busted twigs and mud, along with the trail of bloodied grass – seemed to be staring back at them with the ferocity of a flashing blue light already perched on top of it.

He looked at Eddie.

'No,' he said. The only answer he could give, but allowing Eddie the opportunity to replace the gun in the waistband of his trousers, and consider his next move.

Within seconds Eddie had turned away and was already making his way back toward the trees just above the stream.

John watched him momentarily before following his example – heading the other way – making his way back across the field.

At halfway he had the option of running; he would probably have made it – but somehow it didn't seem necessary, or appropriate. And, fact was, there was little need. By then Eddie was halfway along the stream on his way back to the pipe.

Only when he reached the gate, did he move a little more quickly along the path toward civilisation.

✻ ✻ ✻ ✻ ✻

Entertaining

Carl Warburton leant casually against the kitchen unit, watching his wife, Kim, chopping onions. It was an ideal position for viewing her – the lithe willowy body – supple and snake-like – particularly endearing in the plastic pinny, with its connotations of uniform, and a stern rebuff to anyone likely to try interfering with her. She made a point of feigning ignorance of her husband's presence, resolved to devoting her attention to the bald kernels of silvery flesh.

He stood a while, eyeing the gin rotating round the twin boulders of ice until his resistance finally cracked and he sidled up to her, easing his hand around her waist, bubbling tiny 'o's in the warmth of her neck.

Her flimsy protests served only to draw him closer and the knife to drive more ferociously through the next slice of onion, her movements as much with him as from him as he gyrated himself gently against her buttocks.

'What are you making?' He was pointedly leaning over her shoulder, attempting to show some interest in the goings-on on the counter.

'Just a few chicken tikka drumsticks,' she said, dunking the onion rings in a Pyrex dish.....'Bit of salad....and profiteroles.'

'What's profiteroles?' he asked, his fingers closing idly round her right breast, making a play for the taut bead lying somewhere at its summit.

'You know what profiteroles are....And there'll be fresh fruit salad....and then coffee....'

He planted a final smudge on the nape of her neck and returned to the gin.

'You're going to a lot of trouble,' he said – speaking as much to himself, raising the glass to view his wife through the jagged reflections of light. He eyed the lumps of chicken heaped at the ready in an adjacent dish.

'It's only a few bites on sticks.' She turned her attention to the tikka-mix, rotating it to a loose enough texture to be placed into a second Pyrex bowl.

He slid more gin around the ice-blocks, observing the fuzzy swirls floating round the slices of lemon.

She reached across to take two oranges from a bowl.

Matthew and Sue were to be their guests for the evening; a couple they'd recently met who lived over in Beckenham, some five or six miles away. She – twenty-five – brunette – nice legs – Trainee Officer for the new branch of Tescos that had opened in the Parkway Precinct. Matthew was a few years older – making in-roads in the carpet-cleaning business with moves towards a more generic 'Home-Care Management' service via internet links. They'd met on one previous occasion and whilst her welcome had certainly raised an eyebrow, it appeared to have gone down well, and once the preliminaries were done and dusted, they'd pretty much hit it off straightaway.

Dish at-the-ready for the oven and a glass of red poured into a waiting glass, she shuffled towards him and popped a playful kiss on his cheek – brief compensation for her earlier rebuff. She reached to the cupboard to withdraw four cut-glass dishes and some small silver-bordered side-plates.

'Do you like Sue?' The question was popped casually between putting the finishing touches to a spread of lettuce leaves and arranging space for the bowl on the formica top.

He rattled the glass, watching the ring of lemon as if the answer to her question lay somewhere in its tiny concentric movements.

'She's okay,' he said, 'Nothing special.' His attention was drawn to outside, beyond the garden fence, where his neighbour was indulging in his favourite past-time of pushing his fucking lawn-mower up and down neat orderly lines of his billiard-table garden.

Which was true. She was pleasant enough – a little over-eager to 'amuse' – as is the norm on these occasions – probably nerves – something to do with being a stranger venturing on alien territory; they'd invited them round to their place for the evening rather than schlepping all the way out of town.

'Nothing more then?' His wife turned her attention back to the glasses.

He pursed his lips as if not entirely decided. Then he smiled. 'Nothing more,' he said.

She raised her lips and they kissed more fully, the plates temporarily forgotten.

'And what about Matthew?' asked Carl, relaxing his grip on his wife to eye next door where a frenzy of shaking what looked like roots or black triffidy-looking things appeared to be cause for consternation. 'How do you find him?'

'He's okay…'

She placed the last dish on the counter and turned her attention to a pack of profiteroles.

He abandoned the neighbours to return his attention to the contents of his glass.

About seven-o-clock would be time to get ready for the evening, though the preparations would begin well in advance – laying the gear out on the duvet just to check that everything was ready and in its place. Any last minute adjustments needed time to be sorted and previously-unnoticed flaws time to be spotted before it was too late.

For her it would be a slit plaited skirt, thighs bared, slightly baggy streak-patterned blouse with just a modicum of puff in the sleeves, bright orange sash and earrings purchased from a street market in Spain last year. And for him: black strides – worn to be a little too baggy, and a faintly checked shirt, open necked, worn outside the trousers.

The drinks were sorted; a few poppy lagers cooling next to the *Muscadet* and the profiteroles and the next gin bottle ready and waiting on the kitchenette.

He was relaxing on the sofa, drawing on his Consulate-Cool cigarette and listening to the clitter-clatter of last minute activity in the kitchen.

It was just before eight-o-clock that the phone rang.

His wife returned a few moments later her arm rested against the jamb. Her crestfallen expression told its own story.

'You'll never guess,' she said.

'What?' He draped an outstretched arm over the top of the settee and turned to face her.

'They're not coming.' The announcement – outwardly calm and controlled – was heavy with indignation. She lowered her eyes to the floor, absently stubbing a high-heeled toe in the space beneath her feet.

'Why....What's the problem?'

'She says she's feeling a bit under the weather.'

'Oh....right.' He shook the glass and drew his feet into a sitting position on the sofa.

'You don't seem too bothered,' she said, still standing at the door, struggling to find the composure to move in and join him.

'I'm bothered,' he said...'Don't get me wrong...I'm definitely bothered.'

He looked across to where his wife was stood head-bowed at the door – her toe still flirting with the tuft of carpet. He allowed her a moment's contemplation and then tapped the sofa cushion into place at his side. He patted the cushion.

'Come on....sit down.'

She stiffened – reluctant to compromise her sense of indignation. Only at her husband's repeated request did she take her place at his side. He spoke as one might when disclosing a family tragedy to a child.

'Look, I know you've been to a lot of trouble....but I did warn you didn't I?'

He reached an arm in an attempt to pull her closer, but she wasn't yet ready to be consoled. It was his turn to sigh.

'It's so thoughtless,' she said. 'I don't see why people have to be so inconsiderate.' She turned to her husband, her fingers fumbling idly in her lap.

'I don't want to see them again.' He smiled and drew her closer. 'I shouldn't worry on that score – I expect that was the message they were trying to convey.'

Her eyes turned to the kitchen, where the chicken... profiteroles....fruit-salad – once ready to take pride of place on the table – were already looking at the waste bin.

'Look they're gone now and we'll forget they ever existed.... okay....Come on, it's only food – it can be frozen or put in the fridge.' He reached to her, trying to draw her from her sense of indignation.

She finally relented, welcoming his hand rising to her shoulder, where it hesitated a moment, before lowering to her left breast. She let it laze there a while and then he spoke in little more than a whisper.

'Wait here....I'll be back......'

He left the room to return a minute or two later holding a magazine. Having regained his seat next to her he laid it across their adjacent knees, opened at the appropriate page. She listened quietly as he read, following the words with his finger. 'Right.....Well that's Sue and Matthew so we can forget that one. Now....how about....

'Let's meet and 'swop ideas' – full range of toys to meet all needs ....your place or ours – no time wasters'

or maybe....

'I think I like your hubby – watch him take me from all angles' ...have photos....D.I.Y. and 'O'.

Or... how about...

'Babes' bath-time'....two in a tub – rubbedy rub......soap me, spank me...
and finally fuck me...Anything goes... your place or ours... discretion guaranteed...'

He paused – placing the magazine to one side on the cushion – trying to catch her eye.
'See....have a little faith in people.....Come on....have a browse, pick one and we'll follow it up tomorrow.'
He made his way to the kitchen to refill his glass whilst she took the magazine and began to browse her way down its contents. On his return, she pointed at a lower part of the page. He read it and nodded.
'Right...okay....We'll go for it.....Now.....I'm feeling a bit peckish – got anything to eat?'
She stroked his cheek.
'I expect I can come up with something,' she said.
    Before she rose from her seat, he squeezed her arm and pulled her towards him.
'I love you,' he said.
'I love you too,' she replied and they kissed fully and uncompromisingly before she went to replenish her glass and check the oven.

Extracts From
'A Northern Childhood'

'It was the simple moments that we cherished the most.'

One of the things me, Oggie and Wainthrop had in common was fancying Panther's mam. Panther had some o' that dark blood in 'im from Spain or Italy or some said it was Costa Rica (that's how he came to be called Panther.) It gave 'im that dark edge to his skin that made a lot of the girls fancy 'im. Panther's mam – she were a different class. She looked like one o' them big tittied women in't pictures on the front of paperback books that you reckoned might be mucky (but when you went through 'em, weren't that mucky at all.) They generally had big muscles and sometimes wore a kind of leather skirt like a gladiator. We used to nick a few 'o them books from Gregory's in town, cos Gregory – the bloke who owned the shop – didn't know his arse from 'is elbow; they reckoned he had some long-term damage to 'is 'ead. He'd be looking down at't floor most of the time, mumbling to his trousers. Anyway we'd nick a few books wi' big tittied women on't front and then get back round our way and start flicking through 'em for good bits, but there weren't hardly any 'good bits' in 'em, and they weren't that 'good' either – some of 'em were shite – not worth nickin', ne'er mind buying.

'There's nowt but shite in my one,' Wainthrop 'd come out with, leafing through't pages to find bits wi' bare titties in 'em. Once we got to know more about books, we got to realise that the best ones had blank covers, maybe pink or purple with no pictures on the front except maybe a pencil line drawing and titles like 'She' or 'Lace' or a bird's name like 'Melanie' or 'Cindy'. Anyway, Panther's mother looked like one o' them big tittied women on t' other books. But he used to get a bit touchy if you talked to 'im about it. Like when we were out on't bikes and we'd take a break from riding and be lazing around on a bit o' grass and pick a piece for chewing and one of us'd just come out with it.

'Tell you what, I could do a number on your mam Panther,' one of us'd say, staring up at the sky, chewing a blade o' grass, trying to look tough and nonchalant like lads in the latest film. 'Gi'oer, that's my mam you're talking about,' he'd say, sounding all hurt and leaning on 'is elbow and looking across. 'Oh don't take on; we're only talking about it,' Oggie'd say, 'What's fuss? I wish I 'ad a mam with a pair on 'er like your mam.'

'You shouldn't go round fancying people's mams,' Panther'd say. 'Birds are for fancying, not mams.'

'All wi saying is she's got a nice pair on 'er, that's all,' Wainthrop'd add, trying to keep the peace. 'Firm set of jugs that's all.' He'd sit up and twiddle his fingers above his belly, to illustrate his point.

'Give o'er,' Panther 'd say, lying back and looking pained. 'It's my mam you're on about.'

For a while he'd lie there pulling bits of grass away from the kerb-side and kicking splays of gravel around with his right foot. '"t ain't right.'

'Oh give o'er,' Oggie'd pipe up again. 'Trouble wi' you is you think too much. Stop worrying. It's only a pair o' jugs.' There'd be a lull as Panther'd turn away again still looking a bit peeved, despite Oggie's attempts to build bridges.

'Come on, let's go 'n get berry guns and go round on't bikes,' I'd say, getting quickly to my feet, sensing that maybe Panther's mum'd best be given a bit of a wide berth for a while and that we needed to make a move. Panther'd still be looking a bit sulky as he climbed to his feet. But he'd brush himself down and take hold of his bike and as we'd get ready to wheel ourselves off the kerbside he'd be concentrating on getting his foot on 't pedal it'd all get to be forgotten. As we'd get to our feet, Oggie'd give his saddle a quick slap to shift any gravel that might have found its way there.

'Anyway..'doing a number on 'er, don't necessarily mean givin' her a good shagging,' he'd say, pulling his left leg over the crossbar and wheeling away from the kerb.

Berry guns were guns that fired little green berries, but they were seasonal – only any use when berries were hard and green enough. They were made of wood and elastic stretched round a trigger affair. The knack was to make one without getting any splits in the wood. Splits in the wood could become obsessive.

You could have a gun that fired okay but if there were any splits you'd smash it to bits and start on another. Once we'd made 'em, we needed summat to fire 'em at. Sometimes it'd be tins or street lamps or kids skulking round ends of their paths or sitting on walls. Best thing were firing 'em at Cheryl Warburton's arse.

Cheryl Warburton lived at end house and sometimes liked a laugh. I don't know who came up wi' idea, probably Oggie, but anyway we told 'er we needed summat to fire at other than tin cans or little kids, so why didn't she bend o'er a wall wi' 'er knickers down so we could fire at 'er arse? She got a bit moany about it at first and sulked and reckoned it wa'nt fair, so we said we'd pay 'er. But she said it wa'nt the money, she just wan't sure whether she wanted to. We couldn't see what all the fuss was about – it was only berries – it wan't bullets. Anyway she came round in't end, but we had to play away from 'er 'ouse cos once 'er mam were looking through't window once and when she saw 'er Cheryl 'anging o'er't wall wi' 'er skirt 'itched up and her knickers down and us firing berries at 'er arse she come out and give us a bollockin'. She called us 'dirty little bastards', but she were wrong there cos there were nowt 'dirty' about it. Anyway we'd to go a few streets away and get 'er to bend o'er and whip 'em down there. She'd tell us to 'urry up and get a move on' but we told 'er to stop moaning and to stand still. Best way we did it was – we'd wait till she were bendin' o'er t' wall and then get on our bikes at end 't street and get guns ready and ride past in line, one by one, firing at 'er arse, like in cowboy films. We'd miss most 't time but we sometimes managed to score. You got a point for every 'hit'. She used to complain when one of us got a 'hit' cos she reckoned it stung, but we told 'er to stop moaning – that was the idea.

Oggie had one shot and it lodged in't crack above 'er arse. We only knew when she shouted 'Oi that 'urt'. Closer inspection confirmed that the berry was still there, lodged firmly inside the crack. We'd 'eeny meeny miny mo' to see who'd get to take it out. Oggie moaned like fuck saying it were 'im who'd fired it up there so it should be 'im who'd get to fag it – but Wainthrop said we should all get a chance and anyway Oggie wanted to take it out wi' 'is teeth, and Cheryl said he couldn't cos that was being a 'dirty bastard'. In't end she took it out 'erself to stop all't arguing.

Sometimes if it were just one of us out with Cheryl on our own, she'd let you muck around with 'er 'private parts' for a while, but we 'ad to get well out o' way for that, down by't railway bridge or round one o't bends in the river. And you'd to promise not to tell anyone too, which we did, so as no-one 'd think we were dirty bastards.

On Sundays it were church. I 'ated it. I 'ad to get dressed up. Jeff The Plank, who lived down our street and had a big fat cat that were about as fat as a beach-ball, used to go to church every Sunday in 'is jeans – said 'e wanted God to see 'im normal and not putting on airs and graces'. We used to call him 'Jeff The Plank' because he always used to stand bolt upright and lean back when he were walking. I told mam I'd be goin' to church in jeans so as not to let God see me putting on airs and graces, but she cuffed me and said 'did I think God was daft, or what?'

The new church was the ugliest building for miles. Just a big pile 'o red bricks. Near 't top there were coloured glass windows with pictures of chubby kids poking each other with toasting forks. I'd always fancied taking 'old 't fork and pitchin'it straight into't little cherub with the puffy cheeks and then roasting 'im over a fire; that'd take smirk off his face. Every time I walked through that church door I got that strange feeling, like dentists or stepping into a derelict mill or a hospital, you're frightened to raise your voice and you feel chilly.

They had a picture of Jesus on the wall. He had a pale face and long hair and big eyes. He was standing in front of a long table where other people were sitting who looked a bit like him. One o' teachers at school'd said that Jesus was probably black (or brown anyway). When I told mam that Jesus was black she cuffed me and told me not to blaspheme. I'll tell that teacher when I see 'im he talks a load of bollocks.

We sang a hymn about God being kind and loving everyone and then said a prayer for people who'd died in an earthquake in Pakistan. We prayed that rescue people'd get to 'em in time or at least get to 'em *some* time so they could be buried proper. And we prayed for their 'loved ones'- I think that's relatives who are dead. Then there was a prayer for a girl who lives round t' corner, who's spent her life in splints cos of a brittle bone disease – the vicar thanked God for giving her courage and a special splint that lets her bend her leg and straighten it again.

Then the bag came round. Everyone looked at it before it got to 'em like they were thinking maybe they could nick it and swop it for one wi' buttons in, or maybe nick some of it. You'd to put some money in it cos the church din't have much money. I sometimes wondered about that cos the vicar's 'ouse were big enough; and I sometimes thought about taking some money out for Oggie's mam cos she were even poorer than 't church. Oggie's arse were only a couple o' stitches from poking' out of 'is kecks most days.

You couldn't even get away after the service; you'd to wait around till mam and dad 'd stopped talking. Sometimes it'd be with Jim and his wife Betty. Jim was loaded; made 'is money out o' sellin' plastic turds and Whoopie cushions. They made 'em up in a factory in Darwen – I got one o 't turds; he give it me for nowt, but it wan't much good; it werent wrinkly enough, so I give it my sister for 'er birthday. He give me a Whoopie cushion too, but it's more or less lost its fart cos main seam's got a bit frayed down one side. Anyway he was saying how they were taking over some other shop in Wigan where they had all that sort o' stuff and new ones too. Latest were a doll that could piss – all you did was pour water in its 'ead and then press down on it.

He said they were well on 't way to starting up and they'd only 'ave to sack a few from 't other shop, which wa'nt too bad considering how much money they'd be making out of it, and some of 'em might get other jobs in any case.

His wife Betty had a shop that sold wheelchairs to handicapped people. She was saying how you wouldn't believe what they can make these days – there were chairs for if you'd got arms or legs missing and there were another one that were for them whose got their arms *and* legs missing – she reconed you steered it with your teeth; but they only had the one in stock, so they were hoping they wouldn't get a rush on with Christmas coming, or they'd 'ave to order some more from Cleveleys, which would take a while cos of the strike.

Then they said 'ow it'd been a good service and 'simple', not too 'fussy' - that's what they liked about this church. You didn't 'ave to be thinking about it all't time; just turn up Sunday and then you can go 'ome and do what you like for't rest of the week – not like some o' these religions, where they keep on at you all't time, driving you mad.

Anyway, we'd finally get away 'n get 'ome so's mam and dad could 'ave a good row over Sunday dinner. They always had a good row after church. Sometimes it'd be a bloody good row and they'd really lay into each other. No-one really knew what it were about, apart from fact they didn't get on – which they never 'ad anyway, so why bother rowing about it. Anyway, it was their business – nowt to do wi' me. I'd get to kick my ball around in't garden or maybe get to go round Panther's and 'ave a sken at 'is mam or maybe spend an hour wi' Cheryl Warburton down't railway bridge.

Worse than Sunday mornings were Sunday afternoons. It was 'visiting grandma' time. Grandma was okay, she were a kindly soul with cheeks like blancmange that went squidgy when you give 'er a peck on't cheek.

When we got round 'er 'ouse, she'd be standing in't kitchen in brown stockings wi' legs like two brown drain-pipes, that folded out over her ankles and shoes. Her sisters 'ad the same sort o' legs, so maybe it was summat to do wi' their hormones. Grandad'd be in his chair. He never said much; in fact 'e never said owt, except 'spend a match' when 'e wanted a match lit to light his pipe. He was a thin bloke with a long bony face and a huge snorkel that always had a big fat droplet on't end, like a tap.

I'd never quite got the 'ang of 'love'. I couldn't always figure out what it meant. I knew what it meant wi' girls like Julie Grundy in our class at school. I loved Julie Grundy and I'd tell 'er so loads o' times when I were snoggin' 'er in't long grass up Sandhills. I knew I were supposed to love grandma and grandpa too, but I couldn't really figure out what it meant with 'em; she were a kindly soul, like I say, but I wan't going to snog 'er in't long grass. In fact we'd nowt much in common – she wan't going to come out wi' us firing berry guns at Cheryl Warburton's arse or play 'head football' or 'three and your in'. She put plenty o' syrup on 'er syrup sandwiches, I'll give 'er that; like I say, she were a kindly soul.

Sometimes, Saturdays, I'd have to go round to Molly and Missie, who were two sisters or maybe it was twins, who lived

in Samson Street round the back of Whalley Road and 'ardly
ever left 'ouse. They always seemed to be dunkin' washing in a
bowl or wringing it out in a bowl or piling it up at the side or
makin' flour or doin' somethin' in a bowl. And all't time they'd
be talking in these sharp screechy-type voices wi't volume on
full and chomping their teeth.

They were both well on the fat side and kind of waddled when
they walked in and out o't scullery. They'd a funny habit o'
takin' a line each in turn when they were saying owt, so you'd
to be following' 'em backwards and forwards like a tennis ball
if you were listening to 'em. They'd a much younger brother or
some reckoned it were a son 'o one of 'em done in secret.
Anyway he were called Eccles and spent most of 'is time
walloping 't dog – a cocker spaniel – with this little brush thing
that moved in and out of a copper tube. He were a short-arse
which were perhaps why he liked walloping things. They'd
sometimes tell 'im for 'itting dog, but it never made no
difference and they were often too busy moaning about folk
who they didn't like, which were most folk; particularly posh
folk.

I'd gone round to take a box o' kitchen stuff mam said they
could 'ave and as soon as I were in't living room they were
moaning about weather while they were up to' elbows in soap
suds. Eccles were skulking around by't kitchen door looking
mean wit' brush in 'is hand.

'Get out 't road,' one of 'em 'd say, givin' 'im a push when they
went back into't kitchen to get a bit more washing – They'd
push 'is head away wi' big porky arms. Then't dog'd appear
and Eccles'd be watchin' it like a hawk.

'You'll know Connie Entwhistle. Lives up Ferzackerly Street,'
Maisie says, mashin' a pair o' leggings out in't washin' bowl.

'They've gone and done it,' says Millie, rinsing' a cardi out
over't sink.

'Done what?'

'Movin',' says Maisie, pushing Eccles out o't road and twisting
leggings in her fist.

'Wilmslow way,' says Millie, plunging' t cardi back into 't sink and chompin' 'er teeth.

'To be wi' posh folk,' says Maisie, grabbin' a pile o' woollies and takin' 'em to't scullery.

'And fancy folk,' says Millie, takin' 't pile o' woollies off Maisie and scowlin' at Eccles. 'Get out o't road.'

'Don't want to be with us normal folk no more.'

'Ordinary folk like us.'

'Want to be wi' la-di-da' s'.

'And Fancy Dans.'

Next thing – dog appears from under't window so Eccles takes hold o' brass brush thing and gives it a good wallop on't 'ead, sendin' it yelping and scurrying away across carpet. Then he'd be after it wi' his hand up in't air ready.

'Leave it,' I'd say. I wan't too keen on seeing dog gettin' clobbered every time it showed its face. 'It's doin' you no 'arm.'

'Bollocks 'es my dog. Come 'ere you bastard,' he'd say.

'Oh leave 'im be,' Maisie 'd say, from't scullery, foldin' 't washin' and layin' it in a pile by't cupboard. I didn't know whether she were on at me or Eccles, but she were looking towards Eccles.

'Keep on harassing 't dog. What's up wi' yer?'

'I'll 'ave it,' says Eccles, looking round back of sofa to see if 'e' were still skulking there.

'Should get yourself a girlfriend 'stead o' wallopin' dog,' says Millie, hangin' a pair of stockings on't line.

'Bit o female company's what you need,' says Maisie.

'Nice posh girl from down south…down London way,' says Millie, 'do you 't world o' good.'

'Who talks like the Queen.'

'All la di da and silky knickers.'

'Not like us ordinary folk.'

'That's what you need.'

There were a sudden shout from Millie as water comes splashin' over 't side of bowl. She'd step back to avoid it and swear at bowl..and Eccles. 'Now look what you've made me do.' Still scowling, she'd turn to look at me.

'Do you want summat to eat?' She'd be takin' her apron off to
wring it out over 't bowl.
'We've fresh-made parkin,' says Maisie.
'Or chocolate cake,' says Millie
'I'll 'ave a bit o' chocolate cake,' says I.
'It's over in't cake tin, next to't rollin' pin – help yourself,' says
Maisie.
'I'll 'ave some too,' says Eccles, abandoning't brush for a while
and making his way into the scullery.
They made some decent chocolate cake the pair of them,
I'll give 'em that. Chocolate were firm – like real chocolate
on top and all't cream sort of squidged out when you ate it.
I loaded a plate and looked around for a fork to be eatin' it
with.
'Where's forks?'
'What do you want forks for?' says Millie, stuffin' a shirt
through't mangle that they used for dryin' stuff.
'To eat cake with.'
'Give o'er wi 'you. Get it in yer fist.'
'We don't use forks for eatin' a bit 'o cake round 'ere,' says
Maisie
'Forks are for pansies,' says Millie.
'And posh folk,' says Maisie,
'You're not a posh person are you?'
'Or a pansy?'
'Get it in yer fist and stop whingeing,' says Millie
'Take it in yer fist, like ordinary folk,' says Maisie.
It were pretty good cake I'll give 'em that, though 'alf of it
dropped out on't floor when it squidged through my fingers.
That got dog back from round side o't chair sort o sniffin' and
poking' 'is 'ead into't scullery and Eccles reaching for 'is brush.
Dog were just helping' 'imself to a few bits o' cake when – twat!
– he'd get another walloping on't 'ead.
'Take that you bastard,' says Eccles, looking all proud like and
looking down at dog that'd gone scurrying round back o' t
settee.

'Oh, give it berth,' says Maisie.

'Get yourself a girlfriend,' says Millie.

'You vicious sod,' says I, looking a bit aggrieved and looking out for 't dog behind the chair.

'It's only a bit 'o fun,' says Eccles grinning, still waving' the brush in't direction o' dog in one hand and reachin' for't chocolate cake in't other. 'He don't mind.'

When I left, they give me a big hunk o' chocolate cake, so I wa'nt complaining. I were goin' to pat dog on the 'ead but it belted off round back o settee as soon as it saw me coming near him. Didn't 'ave much of a life that dog.

Night time were always 't same round our 'ouse. I'd get to watch a bit o' telly and when a pop singer or anyone wi' long hair come on, dad'd point at screen and shout about 'ow 't lads in 'is regiment in't army would o' beat shit out of 'im if they'd o' got 'old of 'im.' And mam'd be busy ironin' or summat and when she'd come in't room, she'd take a fag from packet on't mantelpiece, stand up straight and kind o' lean back a bit and let a real long rasping fart go.

She really knew how to fart did mam – it wan't just a short little popping one or a 'one second wonder' – it were a great long rasping bastard that must 've lasted all o' five seconds – it'd come out like tearing a ten foot length of carpet. But she always wasted 'em on us – she'd sometimes drop one when Uncle Horace – who never did owt or liked owt, on grounds o' coming from Bacup – were round. Like he'd not eat Chinese food or owt like that 'foreign muck' – 'not wi' comin' from Bacup.'

But apart from Uncle Horace, all mam's farts were wasted cos she'd never let one go when Oggie or Wainthrop were round.

I'd plead with 'er, 'Aw go on mam let one go for Oggie and Wainthrop, they'd love it. But she'd just cuff me round 't 'ead and tell me not to be so filthy. I'd say it's not filthy, it's nature, but she'd never listen. I'd 've scored loads o' points for 'aving a mam who farted like that....but she just didn't seem to understand. I suppose that's mams for you. They only ever think o' themselves.

Note: We weren't serious about 'doin' a number' on Panther's mam. None of us would've known where to start – apart from Nobby Sidebottom who were shaggin' everything in sight from 'bout age o' ten.

* * * * *

['fag it' - 'Sixties' South Lancashire dialect for 'getting something back – retrieving something.'
  'kecks' - 'trousers' 'sken' - 'look'.]

Four Men in a Bar

The Green had retired into darkness for the day; the dotted benches and pathways home only to a teenage couple and a few stray cats with an eye for the night air.

You walked down the lane that bordered The Green, past a number of houses until you reached the small iron fence that ringed The House itself, which was set well back from the lane.

A manor house in some past existence – it had a huge front with towering pointed gables, set in a few acres of neatly tendered lawns, towering oak trees and geometrically arranged gardens. Though a little faded these days and in need of some restoration and renovation, its 'inner sanctum' still held a kind of 'period appeal' comprising a number of spacious rooms connected by a warren of hallways and stairs. A small gate from the lane led the way down a crazy paving path which took you to a large old front door past the tiny office and into the passageway along the ground floor to The House bar at the front end of the building.

The bar was small and basic and had been recently decorated in a questionable shade of pastel orange and illuminated by a series of tiny wall lights. A faded picture of the Queen, the one where she still looked fresh and vaguely virginal, hung on the far wall next to the fire-extinguisher.

Bill stood leaning against the bar, one foot propped on the foot rail, nursing his pint of non-descript keg bitter. He was staring at the spirit optics attempting to read the labels on the side of the bottles. George, the barman, stood a few yards to his right, humming a tune vaguely reminiscent of *'Danny Boy'* as he gently rotated a raised wine glass against the orange wall light. He placed the glass down on the counter and took the next from the drip tray.

George was a stickler for things, particularly 'procedures'. There was a 'way of doing things' and he stuck to the way of doing these things, as a matter of both principle and pride. He was at that moment, in the process of demonstrating the 'procedure' for cleaning glasses to anyone who cared to watch. It had been some fifteen or so years ago that he had taken the post of 'barman' at The House; the neat orderliness of the Community Centre Bar seeming a more likely forum for establishing and maintaining his standards than the slap-dash approach of your average High Street pub. It was just a shame that the beer was crap.

As Bill continued his attempt to read the labels on the bottles, George passed the scrim cloth over each glass, applying the correct motion and correct degree of pressure, before lining it neatly on the counter under the bar, next to the half-pint glasses. His face was round and ruddy, and gave an impression of slightly folding in on itself at the centre, as if succumbing to some powerful surge of internal suction.

'Jim in tonight?' he asked, placing the cloth on the back counter and reaching down for a carton of fruit juices to be placed on the cold shelf.

'Yeh...He'll be in,' said Bill, his face still fixed on the bottles. He turned an eye towards George.

'Is that ginger wine you got there on the right?' He had abandoned the effort to read the labels from where he was standing and his eye had been caught by a green bottle towards the right end of the line.

'Which one?' George moved to his right and pointed up at the line of bottles.

'That one there on the end,' said Bill, stabbing his finger in the direction to the right of the optics.

'This one?'

'Yeh. That one.'

'It's called Wormwood. Halfway between a wine and a liqueur. It's got a spicy, aromatic edge to it. Quite pleasant actually.'

'I like a ginger wine Christmas day, just after the meal. Sit back, feet up, very nice,' said Bill, leaning back, recollecting the moment with a degree of self-satisfaction.

'Especially on a chilly day,' said George. 'Long walk over the forest. Back lunchtime. Feet up...as you say...very nice, keeps out the chill.'

'What I like is that edge; it's got that edge to it,' said Bill.

'That's right.'

'What's the other one? What's it called?' Bill tapped the bar, his forehead furrowed in thought. It was always frustrating when you had the name of something right there on the tip of your tongue.

'Which one?' asked George, holding a glass up to the light to observe the diamond sparkle he had brought to its surface.

'The other one,' said Bill.

There were no other customers in the bar; there rarely were these Thursdays. There were very few people in the whole building. The only activities running at the moment were the 'Embroidery' women up on the first floor, 'Watercolours' in the end room and the 'Anarchist' guys.

Only occasionally would someone pop down to return a glass or maybe pick up a tea or coffee. For the most part, little stirred, rather like a museum that had finally closed its doors to the public. George hummed another verse of *Danny Boy* as he continued to peer into the star-like refractions in his next glass.

'Mind you, you pay so much for drinks these days, you wonder where the money goes,' said Bill. 'I was in town with my wife on Monday and we went in this little wine bar-type place, ordered two glasses of wine...Three pounds seventy five a glass. Three pounds seventy five!' he repeated, his exasperation as clear as one of George's glasses.

'Ridiculous,' said George, rotating the glass one last time against the light and nursing the cloth gently across its surface.

'Same everywhere now mind.' He placed the glass on the shelf next to the others.

There was a movement in the corridor and eyes turned as Jim arrived. Though well into his 'senior' years, there was still something of a 'boyishness' about old Jim, in his pacey, slightly pigeon-toed walk and a pre-occupation with war, battle ships and fast cars – issues, sadly, of little interest to those whose company he shared. As he approached the bar he offered a raise of the hand and moved with some pace to the coat hooks to hang his jacket. He still boasted a thick head of hair which, though almost pure silver in hue, ebbed and waved like a youthful Rockabilly from the fifties. He gave the quiff a customary pat as he took his place at the bar.

'So how's old Jim?' said Bill, half turning towards him.

'Can't complain I suppose. Traffic's bad down by the roundabout. Must've been some accident.' He was attempting to disengage his foot which had somehow become entangled with the stool leg and the foot rail. He reached for a tissue from his pocket.

'There was an accident last week just up the M11,' said George, taking a glass by the stem and holding it to the light. 'Car travelling one direction crossed the central reservation and collided with a lorry travelling the opposite direction; could have been very nasty.'

'Yes well that's motorways,' said Bill. 'The trouble with some drivers once they get on a motorway is they don't think.' His eyes continued to scour the bottles lining the spirits shelf. 'They think 'right, I'm on a motorway now; I can relax – no need to think."

'Especially youngsters,' said George.

'Youngsters are the worst for not thinking,' said Bill, 'Too pre-occupied with other things.'

George nodded.

'Thing is with youngsters,' said Jim, finally extricating his foot and seeking to ease himself into a comfortable position on the stool. 'To them, a car's a symbol of manhood. Like a prick. Every time they're driving a car, it's like they're screwing a woman.'

'That's right,' said George, 'that's why there's so many accidents.'

Bill nodded, raising his glass to his lips. 'Bloke next door to us driving up Woodford, a dog ran in front of his car, he swerved, hit a lamppost. Couldn't see the dog at all,' he said.

'Till he swerved' said Jim.

'Well, till just before he swerved,' said Bill.

'By which time it was too late,' said George, holding the glass by the stem and placing it on the shelf.

'Should've run it over,' said Jim, 'I would have.'

'Well that's what he said. Next time, he said, I'm just going to run it over – sod hitting a lamppost.'

'That's right,' said George.

'If he'd been driving the new Five Litre Mustang with a converted RS Turbo he'd've probably squashed it flat before he'd had time to see it or swerve,' said Jim, looking round for confirmation and chuckling.

George discarded the first cloth and leant down to replace it with another from a small cardboard box. He made his way to the beer tap.

'Usual Jim?' he said, reaching under the counter.

'Yeh, I suppose,' said Jim, reaching into his pocket for another paper tissue. He thought he'd brought enough but he was beginning to have his doubts. They all seemed a little on the damp side.

'Jug?'

'Oh yes.'

Jim always drank his beer from a jug; but not to be different or sniffy, but because it simply tasted better. He watched in anticipation as George flicked the lever to release the winsome stream into the jug. He popped the jug on the bar and took the money to the till.

Jim lifted the jug and took a few half-hearted sips at its contents. 'That a ginger wine you got there?' he asked, staring at the green bottle at the end of the shelf. 'I quite like a ginger wine when I'm feeling a bit under the weather.'

'Funny, we were just talking about that,' said Bill. 'I was saying to George, I like it Christmas Day after the meal.'

'It's called Wormwood,' said George. 'It's a kind of wine-liqueur – got a spicy tang, quite aromatic, quite nice actually – especially on a chilly day.'

Jim focused his eyes to see if he could read the label from where he was sitting.

'Think I might have a bottle of Stones at home sitting somewhere in a cupboard,' he said, tentatively folding the tissue and easing it into his pocket. 'I'll have to dig it out when I get back.'

'That's the one...'Stones" said Bill tapping the bar top. 'It was 'Stones' George – the other one.'

'Ah,' said George, taking a glass from the counter. 'We don't actually sell that one, but as you say, it's a popular brand.'

'What's that one called again?' asked Jim, nodding towards the bottle on the shelf and squinting, trying to read the name of it from where he was sitting.

'Wormwood.'

'Go on then, pour me a glass,' he said, flicking open the flap of his wallet and withdrawing a five-pound note.

George made his way over to the spirits and for a moment conversation ceased as eyes followed the procedure for serving the Wormwood. He selected the appropriate glass – much like a wine glass and held it temporarily to the light, twirling it once or twice in his fingers.

He reached for the bottle, removed the top and tipped it slightly to allow a few glugs of thick browny liquid into the glass before placing it down in front of him.

'Now, ideally there'd be a slither or two of ginger in the glass, but unfortunately I can't offer you that,' he said.

'Don't worry about that,' said Jim, abandoning his beer to turn his attention to the Wormwood. He raised his glass to his lips. 'Mm...Oh yes; that's got quite a bite to it, sort of herby taste,' he said, swirling the initial 'taster' round his mouth.

'That's right,' said George, wiping the bottle down and replacing the top.

He was about to pop it back in its place on the end of the shelf, when he was interrupted by Bill's voice.

'Go on George, pour me one.' Bill slapped his hands resignedly on the bar top and reached for his wallet.

George turned with the bottle and lifted a glass from the shelf. Bill watched in anticipation. Jim watched too, perhaps interested to see whether the same quantity was about to be dispensed without the aid of a spirit optic.

'One glass of Wormwood,' said George, placing the glass on the bar.

Bill raised the glass to his lips and under the watchful eye of Jim, took his first sip.

There was a brief hiatus as the liquid registered on his taste buds. He smacked his lips and tongue in an initial appraisal and then approval.

'Mm..Oh yes....Very nice. It's definitely got that spicy edge – that's for sure,' he said, rolling a few more sips around his mouth in confirmation.

'Got a herby sort of taste I reckon,' said Jim, keeping a close eye on Bill's mouth for any subsequent reaction.

'Yes, I see what you mean – it's got a sort of spicy, herby edge to it. Bet it's got a kick to it.' Bill squinted at the bottle to see if he could read the details on the label from where he was sitting.

'It has,' said George, turning the bottle in his hand to read the label.

'Fourteen point five per cent per volume.' He extended his gaze as if checking for accompanying statistics.

'Well if it helps shift this blessed cold, I don't care how strong it is,' said Jim, brushing a near sodden tissue against the rim of his nostrils.

Bill readjusted himself in his seat and held his glass to the light. 'There's something going round,' he said, examining the sparkling effects reflecting in the glass's contents. 'My wife's sister had a cold – coughing, sneezing, sore throat, headache – couldn't shift it for weeks. Must've been a virus or something. Doctor put her on antibiotics. Have you tried Lemsip? that's not bad.'

He stirred the glass in an attempt to establish the exact colour. There seemed to be a touch of green in there somewhere.

Jim raised his own glass to the light to peer into the contents. 'Well I've got to do a bit of shopping tomorrow. I'll pop in the Paki shop and get some. They sell most things down there. And they're always open.'

He swirled the glass gently, eyeing the slow rolling movements. He took another sip and replaced the glass on the counter.

'Amazing what you can get in some of them Paki shops and they put the hours in – you've got to give them that. The shop near us is more like a mini-supermarket; it's open about seven in the morning and still open about eleven o clock at night.' He stopped suddenly to prepare for a sneeze that he felt stirring in the top regions of his nostrils.

'Oh ...they ain't afraid of work,' said Bill. 'Two of 'em got a shop near me, you can buy just about anything. And like you say, you go past there about eleven at night, everywhere else is in darkness except this little shop there still got its lights on. You can say what you like but they put the hours in.'

'Mind you, they're probably selling half the stuff they ain't supposed to be selling,' said Jim, 'you know cut-price fags and booze when they ain't got a licence. Cos they're a crafty lot. A lot of people don't realise it, but they're a crafty lot the Pakis.'

'Yes but they're not hurting anyone Jim. You could look at it that they're providing a service that people want. Good luck to them I say.'

'Oh yeh, I got nothing against 'em shifting a bit of dodgy booze or cut-price fags. If that's what people want, good luck to them.'

'Could end up with a couple of them working behind the bar here, what do you reckon George?' said Bill with a grin.

'Well if they've an eye for work and are reliable, why not? Live and let live – that's my motto,' said George, taking a lemon in one hand and holding the knife horizontally above it.

There is a procedure for slicing lemons – not so thick that they sit in the glass – nor too thin so they become limp and disintegrate in the glass. He held the knife at the correct width and made the first cut.

'You wouldn't get their wives working here mind,' said Jim, watching George's methodical slicing of the lemon.

'No, they draw the line there,' said Bill. 'They are a bit odd when it comes to their women, it's got to be said. The way they stone 'em and that.'

'That's the Muslims,' said Jim sensing another sneeze and quickly opening a tissue to the only dry patch he could find.

'That's right,' said George, popping another slice of lemon into the dish. 'For adultery, even if it's rape.......very peculiar.'

'And the way they dress 'em all in black,' said Bill. 'It's okay if you like dressing in black, you know – if it's your colour, but what if you'd rather wear something a bit lighter – a pair of slacks or a pair of shorts or something in the Summer, seems a bit unreasonable to me. Not to mention getting stoned.'

'Particularly in the heat. Mind you it all comes down to religion; it's very strong out there religion,' said Jim.

'That's the fundamentalists,' said Bill.

'That's right,' said George, holding the knife under the tap before wiping it and popping it back in the cutlery stand.

There was movement in the corridor and eyes turned as a squat-shaped figure made his way towards them; a squat bulbous fellow with a ruddy weather-beaten face. A loose jacket hung from his shoulders and what looked like decades-old dungaree-type leggings flapped round his legs. He wore a pair of old boots which, being unlaced, flopped around his feet, forcing him to walk with a dragging movement, essential perhaps in keeping the footwear in place.

He made his way to the bar and cocked an eye at the others. His arrival drew a temporary halt in proceedings as Jim and Bill acknowledged him with quick nods of the head before returning to their Wormwoods.

'Yes sir?' asked George, abandoning the knife to turn his attention to this most singularly apparelled of customers to have appeared in their midst for some time.

The man spread his hands out in each direction, evidently applying some thought before placing his order.

'I think...I'll have...a..red wine...please,' he said.

As George turned to tend to the drink, the man turned to his left, acknowledging the others with a quick nod of the head. Bill returned the nod, whilst casting an eye over the man's garb, as might the doorman at The Dorchester on the arrival of a transvestite cabaret act.

'Nice little bar,' the man said, acknowledging George on the arrival of the wine.

'A pleasant enough little place,' concurred George, taking the money and depositing it in the till.

The visitor glanced once again to his left, as if contemplating communication, but not quite sure whether it lay within the protocol of The House. Bill, who took some pride in being aware of the various comings and goings in the building, caught his glance and made his decision for him.

'You in one of the classes?' he asked, as if to confirm the guy hadn't just drifted in off the street or come to check the water supply.

'Yes...I am...part of the...political group,' he said, raising his glass to examine the contents before actually taking the plunge to taste it.

'Ah..so you'll be down the end of the corridor on the left past the staircase.'

'Yes..first room on the right...or left....depending on which way you approach it.' He spoke in high-pitched bursts that gave an impression of building to a point of some considerable magnitude. He tipped the glass between his lips and paused a little longer, allowing the full flavour of the wine to register on his taste buds.

Bill leant on the bar gazing in the general direction of the bottles and optics.

'I think that's the room they use for the Spanish class on one of their nights. Always looks to me like a committee meeting's going on there – you know the way all the desks are in a kind of oval shape.'

The man grunted and took in the pastel orange décor of his surroundings, his eyes loitering for a moment on the photograph of the Queen. He returned his gaze to the glass and took another drink.

'We like it that way to avoid implications of seniority, superiority or invitations to assume dominant roles,' he said, smacking his lips in appreciation of what was actually a decent drop of wine, unlike the vinegar that masqueraded under the label in some establishments.

'Mm.. not a bad drop of wine,' he said, with a nod in George's direction.

George nodded and took a few bottles from a box and placed them in the cooler.

Jim had already decided on a refill of Wormwood, prompted by an impression of its likely medicinal qualities.

'So how many of you are there then in the group?' asked Bill, always eager to keep abreast of The House's varied activities.

'Same again George,' said Jim, pushing his glass across the bar and reaching into his wallet.

George moved across the bar and took the bottle from the shelf.

There was some hesitation from the man, as if establishing the exact membership was a far from straightforward business.

'There are…about nine of us…all told. It varies from week to week…but usually… there'd be about nine.'

Bill nodded and turned to catch George's eye.

'And for me George,' he said pushing his glass alongside Jim's. The man watched with interest as George took the green bottle and removed the top.

'What is that you're drinking?' he asked, trying to focus his eyes on the label on the bottle in George's hand.

'It's called Wormwood,' said Bill, 'it's a wine-liqueur, quite spicy; quite nice. It's got that edge to it.'

'Never heard of it,' said the man, raising his own glass to his lips. 'Interesting colour.'

'Two Wormwoods,' said George, placing the glasses on the counter.

Bill handed George the money and turned again to his right.

'So what is it you actually do in this group then...discuss politics or what is it exactly? By the way, I'm Bill, this is Jim and that's George.' He tilted his head towards the other two.

'Harold,' said the man, nodding in response.

Harold paused for a moment, giving the question due thought. 'We...er...explore ways and means...of securing and maintaining meaningful communication ...,' he said, mouthing the words with a degree of precision and care....'That is 'communication'...in the sense of individuals....working with each other...and for each others' shared interests.'

He placed the wine glass on the bar top.

There was a moment's pause as Bill, toying with his glass, turned notions of 'meaningful communication' over in his mind.

Jim raised his glass to the light once more, convinced there was a touch of turquoise in there – maybe it was just the light refracting in the movements of liquid against the glass.

'Well it's interesting that you say that,' said Bill, steadying the glass and looking to his right. 'And I think you're right. I think communication – or 'lack of it' to be more precise – is a big problem when it comes to politics and politicians; you know the way they say one thing and then do the other.'

He spoke with a grimace that seemed to reflect the general disdain of politicians and their innumerable short-comings.

'I mean the way things are going it makes you wonder just what the future holds,' he said, grim-faced and staring hard at the label on the sherry bottle next to the spirit optics.

Harold sat staring vaguely at the bar, his shoulders hunched, his arms folded over a beer towel. He thought for a moment and then finally turned to Bill.

'Communication is... a question... of the individual,' he said. 'You will only find long-term political stability in the abolition of organised authority – non-governmental procedures between free individuals, possibly through syndicalist insurrection or maybe Proudheim's mutualism or through more twentieth century variants of collectivism, demagogic syndicalism and anarchisyndicalism.'

Bill continued to stare hard at the sherry bottle as George reached for a bag of ice and tipped some of the contents into the ice box on the bar counter.

Harold turned to look at his watch. He then took his glass and with a quick flick of the wrist, downed the remainder of the wine, before replacing the glass on the bar. He coughed and stood to straighten his dungarees, brush down his jacket and check his feet were firmly planted between the flaps of his boots.

'Anyway, I must be going,' he said.

He turned to the others, who cast a nod in his direction as he shuffled his way across the bar, pausing briefly in front of the Queen, possibly observing how much she had aged since the picture was taken, before making his way along the corridor to disappear into the night.

Bill and Jim watched George replace the packet of ice in the freezer and slide the last of the lemon slices off the plate into the small bowl.

'Did you get that problem with the carburettor sorted out George?' asked Jim, leaning over the counter to make himself heard as George had just leant down to make a slight adjustment to the cooling machine next to the lager barrel. He re-surfaced a moment later, brushing his hands.

'Eventually. Some problem with a needle or something in the piston. I'm no expert on these things.'

'Could have been some restriction in the fuel flow; maybe they done some re-adjustment in the synchronisation screw,' said Jim.

'Possibly,' said George, taking a glass and giving the lager lever a quick pull.

'They can adjust the synchronisation screw for balancing and controlling vacuum levels,' said Jim looking at Bill who was watching George draw small measures of lager and raise them to his lips.

'Temperamental things cars,' said Bill, taking a mouthful of Wormwood and gliding it over his taste buds.

'Bit like women,' said Jim.

'That's right,' said George, drawing another small quantity of lager and raising it to eye level for examination.

A noise from outside drew their attention and eyes turned simultaneously towards a steady drumming on the windows.

'Rain,' said Jim.

'I should say so,' said Bill. 'Listen to that.'

The rain seemed to increase in ferocity by the second and instinctively the two men slid from their stools and made their way over to the window.

Bill eased the curtain to one side and leant his head close to the glass. Behind him Jim leant forward, his head above Bill's, peering out at the avalanche of bullets descending from the skies. The noise suddenly increased, and for a short time the two stood in silence watching the huge rods smash into the windows and run in thick rivulets down the glass.

'Garden needed it,' said Jim, looking upwards as if to try and spot the source of the onslaught.

'True,' said Bill. 'But I don't fancy walking home in this lot.'

'Stair rods out there George,' said Jim, calling across to George to put him in the picture.

'Seems like it,' said George, standing next to the cooler to gaze in the general direction of the window. There seemed no sign of it relenting.

The two men continued to peer through the streaming glass, barely able to make out the now sodden lawns and rose beds which bordered the path leading to the gate. Beyond the gate, the lane danced and splashed in a torrent of reflections from the orange lamps. The Green beyond was, at that moment, invisible from the bar of The House.

The two resumed their places on the stools.

'Old Harold 'll have got soaked,' said Bill, raising his glass to his lips.

'Probably ended up paddling home,' said Jim.

'Cheers,' said Bill, raising his glass in Jim's direction.

'Cheers,' said Jim, raising the re-filled glass to his lips once more, whilst quickly searching in his pocket for a tissue.

* * * * *

'Gerald's Books'

Gerald Entwistle pushed open the door, triggering the all-too-familiar ring of the bell and made his way almost automatically to the rickety counter at the end of the shop. The two thoroughfares were narrow aisles separated by an apparently random array of cardboard boxes packed to stretching point with paper-and-hard backed books. At their sides, lines of shelves towered to unreachable heights, sagging with the weight of seemingly every word to have been presented in print – Aristotle, Milton, 'Cartography For The Everyman', 'Eclairs And Additional Explorations With Eggs', 'Suffolk Water Fowl', 'Long Summer Days With Alice'….It was all there – just sitting, ready and waiting – mainly waiting. And of course – comics – hundreds of them; every cartoon page that's ever dropped off the rollers, lying-in-wait for the covert cult-fanatics' life-long search for copy number six of 'Eagle', 'Hotspur', or 'Captain Fury And his Howling Commandoes.' And at their side, another box of mags, a quieter lot, this lot – mainly for the guys – the old 'Fiesta's, or its 'sister' – 'Knave'– the horny, down-to-earth ones with your average – or sometimes less than average - 'girl-next-door' look; a better bet for your average punter than the Playboys and Mayfairs, with their highfalutin crap on racing cars stuck in there for respectability and those limp drawn-out 'confessions' at the back that were far too wordy and tame to be bothered with. You wouldn't find the 'hard stuff' though, it wasn't that kind of shop.

Gerald wasn't overly interested in comics, or the books anymore; he was more a roll-your-own fag man and like most practitioners, had – over the years – awarded himself a fair chunk of each day, to perfect the art. As he took his place on his stool he reached for his green Golden Virginia tin and popped it on the table top.

It was a solitary existence, but he had quickly become accustomed to it. People – with their trite conversations and empty platitudes quickly bored him and you didn't get much by the way of customers these days anyway. In years past you'd have had ten to fifteen at a time, browsing, picking, comparing and asking about this book and that book, searching for some musty old number that'd been out of print for about fifty years. But those days were gone. You still got a few characters – the proper 'browsers' – the 'anoraks' and the odd eccentric from time to time. But nowadays it was all done on the 'internet' - you did your browsing on a stool, gazing at a screen, twiddling a plastic lump.

He drew on his cigarette and opened his newspaper.

The doorbell rang. A sharply dressed man with a shiny pink face entered and stopped for a while by the door. This wasn't unusual. Many punters – the non-regulars mainly – often stopped and stalled by the door, as if gauging whether it was worth venturing further.

The man looked furtive, as if seeking somewhere to hide. He looked at Gerald and then looked away as if not to appear rude; and then sidled his way along the aisles glancing up and down as he went, biding his time giving the impression that he had something specific in mind, until he reached the 'adult' mags, where he stopped and quickly flicked through the box – just a cursory glance – before abandoning them for more 'wholesome' pursuits, at a more leisurely pace. He scratched his cheek and looked around vacantly as if not sure quite where to look next, until he finally strode back to the 'dodgy mags' and withdrew three copies.

A glance round confirmed that he was the only customer so he quickly took them to the counter, and paid for them without looking up and without hesitating any longer than it took to be half out of the shop as the money was being popped in the till.

Gerald returned to his paper, popped the fag ash and reached down for his flask. He unscrewed the lid and tipped the warm brown contents into it.

It was ten to fifteen minutes later that the bell rang again and the next customer or potential customer, entered.

He was a middle-aged man with a pair of round, horn-rimmed spectacles perched on a squat, rapidly-balding head. He too paused just inside the door and then once again in front of the shelves on the right. Then, moving slowly, he trailed his fingers along the spines, pursing his lips thoughtfully.

Once at the end of the line, he switched his attention to a different section, not too far away. He certainly gave the impression of having a specific target in mind, unless he too was simply prevaricating before turning his mind to the 'adult' box. Gerald turned the page of his newspaper and took another sip from the flask lid as the man drew near to the counter and turned to speak.

'Don't know if you can help me,' he said, still half gazing at the shelf he had been perusing. He spoke in a quick, clipped voice, quite well-received, with just the slightest trace of the local south east accent.

'I'm interested in Lewis – Matthew Gregory. I don't know if you know off hand if you happen to have anything in stock.'

'Can't say as I do mate. But if you have a browse along that shelf there and the shelf above, you may find something. They're supposed to be alphabetical, but there's always some arse'oles who'll stick 'em back any old place.'

'Okay thanks. 'The Monk's actually the one I'm trying to get my hands on – eighteenth century – classic gothic overtones – probably a spin-off from Walpole's 'The Castle Of Otranto.'

'Well, *if* we've got it it'll likely be somewhere up there like I say, just above where you're standing.'

The man turned to the appropriate section and began to finger his way along the line, just about managing to make out the titles by standing tip toe.

'......which itself purported to be a translation from Italian in 1529. Some claim there are strains of the German Romantics, though I'm not convinced. I've managed to trace some of it. I've been trying to get my hands on some of the dramas. But you know what it's like; needles in haystacks, can't seem to find them anywhere. Still, just got to keep on looking. Seek and ye shall find.'

He continued fingering his way along the shelf, straining his neck considerably in the process. Gerald took another drink of his coffee.

The bell rang and a small bow-legged man wearing a cap entered. He stopped at the door and looked quickly at the counter.

'Aw'right Gerry' he said, with the air of a regular punter.

"Right Pat. What you up to then?'

'Well I was just passing. I've been loading some stuff up over the yard and I thought I'd just pop in and see what's happening.'

'......Some say he had some influence over Scott's earlier poetry though I doubt that, I'd like to see the evidence.'

The man had worked his way along one shelf and was already making in-roads on the one beneath it.

Pat made his way towards the counter brushing his hand affectionately along the volumes on the lower left shelf. When he reached the counter he placed both hands on its edge.

'Right, I'll come clean. I'm after a 'Compton Mackenzie', Pericles; translated from the Greek? I've had a look in the catalogues but I can't trace it no place. Early twentieth Century.'

Gerald drew from his cigarette and cast a casual glance behind him.

'Well I can't recall it being on a shelf, but I've got this box of stuff just behind there, out the back. Most of it's early Greek, Sparta, Zeus, that sort of stuff. I aint had the time to go through it all. But if you want to have a browse help yourself. It's just round by the ladders next to the pile of DIY .

'Cheers. I'll have a quick gander.' He was already halfway into the room, as the first customer approached the counter rubbing his neck and bearing a couple of books.

'Any luck?'

'No, not with the Lewis. But I'll take these two. I like this one; the Huxley 'Mortal Coils'. And the Chekhov.'

'Okay. That'll be two pound eighty....Thankyou.'

'You got some good Athenian stuff here Gerry. I'll take one or two of these.' Pat's voice drifted from the numerous boxed sets waiting in the wings beneath him.

'Take 'em all? Yours for a tenner.'

'Maybe next time. I'll have this one on the Athenian armies. And you got one here on the Hopites and the Boeotians.' Pat turned the copies in his hand, browsing the rear notes for further details.

'Yeh, well. You can 'ave them for three quid.'

'You sure?' He emerged from the rear brushing a few years' dust and debris from his trousers.

'Yeh ...Take 'em.'

He handed a few coins over and with a parting gesture, made his way to the door, pausing briefly to flick through the adult mags on his way.

'You got any strong stuff in 'ere?'

'Nah..Too risky; just your bog standard cock mags.'

'Alright...See you then.'

'Yeh.'

As the door shut Gerry eased himself once again on the stool and reached for his flask. As he unscrewed the lid, he glanced round the shelves at the stacks of spines, and the boxes littering the lower area from the counter down to the window, or what remained to be seen of the window, with two huge cases standing before it. That was the 'Military' section: World Wars, Civil Wars, Napoleonic Wars, The Peloponnesians, The Corinthians, Vietnamese Wars (a few) – a litany of a planet's favourite pursuit squashed like sardines into shelves half the size of a window pane.

And then on the right, a section of a few thousand or so titles of earlier fiction, from Dostoyevsky to Dickens, to the later D.H Lawrence to your Mills & Boone Summer Specials.

He poured the last of his coffee.

In the next hour there were approximately ten visitors to the shop. One departed on hearing the bell, two ventured to the nearest rack, giving it five seconds or so before disappearing. A few browsed for the best part of ten minutes and left without making a purchase and of the remainder, two left apparently unable to locate what they were looking for and he sold a copy of Charlie Buchan's Football Annual from 1964, a tatty copy of 'The Numbers Game; Formats And Established Procedures' and an Ordnance Survey map of a northern section of Suffolk.

In the period that followed business thinned even further, though picked up a little early in the afternoon when the bell announced the arrival of a middle-aged woman who made an immediate beeline for the counter.

He thought at first that he might be dealing with some disgruntled customer come to give him his come-uppance for a dodgy sale. Without hesitation she looked up at him and asked for the Photographic section. She spoke in a strong horsey-type voice, like those from further up the county might speak. He directed her to the Arts below Films/Shows and Artists. She made her way to the shelves and after the briefest of perusals withdrew one, two and then three books, almost without hesitation or examination of their covers or contents.

Her eyes continued to scan the lines as if some in-built radar led her automatically to the targets of her search.

'I see you've got the real stuff,' she announced in a strong horsey voice. 'None of this digital imaging - 'Digital Photography Today' rubbish – The real stuff.'

Her attention turned to the next shelf. There was no response from Gerald. He was accustomed to customers' propensity for thinking aloud without necessarily expecting a reply.

In about a minute and a half she was done and standing in front of the counter with 'The Ilford Graphic Arts Manual – Volume One', 'The Professional Way With Eight Millimetre', 'Polarcolor Today', 'Ornithology before The Lens' and 'The British Journal Of Photography Annual' from 1963.

'Real books.....Real photography.' She reached into her purse. 'Do you know, I've still got my Halina Viceroy with its three aperture and double meniscus f8 lens.'

Gerald took the money and reached for the till.

'And I'll tell you.....It still works!' She took the change and popped it in her purse. 'And I'll tell you what – it still takes a darned fine picture – when I can get the film. Bye.'

Without hesitating or looking round she was off and out of the door.

Gerald sat on his stool, looked at his watch and reached for his bag. He glanced up at the highest columns on the right side of the shop. The upper section read like some divine trek through the ages – Medieval writings, 'Middle England And The Middle Earth', 'Ventures Through Early Ottoman Days', 'Old English Verse': row upon row of dark, dusty blue, grey and brown volumes, as thick as bricks – and permanent as tombstones.

He reached into his bag to take out a small parcel that was his afternoon cheese roll. Unfortunately, he'd forgotten the Branston. He wasn't keen on it without Branston – it reminded him of chewing putty. He put it to one side for a minute and opened his paper.

The bell rang and a man entered with a bag hanging from his left shoulder. He stopped temporarily and then made his way along the right side, scouring the shelves.

'You got a poetry section?' he asked. Gerald directed him to the appropriate shelves on the other side of the shop and part of the top right.

'Ah, thanks.'

The man crossed over and started tracing his finger across the spines. He drew a few copies down from the shelf and flicked through the pages, replacing most of them more or less immediately. One or two he hung onto and placed to one side.

After his initial inspection he returned to the few copies he'd withdrawn and started searching through the pages at a much slower pace with a sense of deliberation, as if determined to gain some reward for his time and trouble.

After a while he appeared to have succeeded, and turned to find Gerald still stationed at the counter.

He prepared himself a moment, half an eye on his audience currently unwinding a slice of clingfilm hooked on his little finger. With book held half aloft he began to read aloud:

'*Heart of the Summer sun strangled in the mire of lower earth lies...rebuked and lost to the sweet eternity of time......*'

Only after appropriate contemplation was the book returned to its place on the shelf.

'Do you take poetry books?'

He had quickly slipped the bag from his shoulder and was already delving enthusiastically into its contents.

'Nah......not any more – don't move 'em much,' said Gerald, hopeful of deflecting the offer that he sensed might be imminent.

'Cos I have a friend who writes, and he put his stuff in little books – properly printed mind,' said the man, unperturbed. Without looking up he withdrew a plastic spine-bound booklet.

'There's some good stuff in 'ere. I told him I'd mention him to you.' Gerald reached for the second cheese roll on the counter and began the business of removing the cling-film.

'Here's one. Do you want to hear it?'

'Not really.'

'Then let me read it,' he continued, deaf – it seemed – to all but the muse. He held the book forward and leant back slightly.

'*I watched you as you scattered your blood in the name of love*
I watched and saw the ooze of your heart become
The lifeblood of your past

I observed you sitting – quietly contemplating
the treasured memories
lying in your lap
like a myriad of golden nuggets.
I saw you cast your eyes
to the sky, the sea and the earth dust.

It's called 'Earth Dust'. What do you reckon?'

'Terrific,' said Gerald, taking a bite from his cheese roll. The man had closed the volume to make a closer examination of its titles.

'Don't worry, there's more,' he said, reopening the book and beginning to get into his stride. This is 'My City'. He paused and leant back.

'My city is my graveyard at night
And my intestined morass by day
I gather my intestines and pile them reddied and bloodied
Like the entrails of a dead dog
To be devoured – methodically and beautifully
Into the dead hours of night

Powerful or what?'

'Stunning,' said Gerald, taking another bite from his roll, but wishing he'd remembered the Branston. The man clicked a tongue in acknowledgement of just how beautiful language can be.

'You can 'ave a volume if you like – I've got one or two spare. My mate said it was alright.' He held the copy out for Gerald to take.

'Nah.....you're alright mate. Don't do much in the way of poems as it goes.'

'You sure?'

'Yeh.'

'Okay – well never mind. If you change your mind, this is my number,' he said, presenting a small card to Gerald as he turned to leave.

He made his way through the door leaving the tinkle of the bell behind him and without buying any of the books. Gerald finished off his cheese roll and threw the crumpled cling-film in the bin.

The clock ticked on. Customers were few and far between and to pass a minute or two, he did a quick calculation of the meagre day's takings so far. As he reached for his paper to return to the crossword, the bell rang and a man entered. He paused to stare round the interior of the shop. He was dressed in a black coat and wore a gaunt lean look that answered to many people's image of Rasputin; a shock of wild hair complementing a short pointed beard protruding from his lower chin. He strode up to the counter and looked Gerald straight in the eye.

'I'm attempting to research 'The Polyphonic Motets Of Lassus' Do you think you can help?' The voice was rich and resonant.

'No idea mate – but I doubt it,' said Gerald.

'Right.'

The man stood a moment as if undecided whether to thank Gerald or admonish him. He turned on his heels, opting for the latter, and made his exit like some bystander disappearing into the mist in a black-and-white film.

He'd started the crossword earlier and as usual was beginning to tire of it. Once he'd done the ones that demanded little exertion he usually abandoned it. He couldn't be arsed after that; you either knew the answers or you didn't.

The bell rang and a man entered. He made a beeline for the section on the right that featured contemporary fiction and began to browse along the titles, seeming at first to have little urge to investigate further. He eventually took 'Games In A Woodland' from the shelf. He turned it in his hand and read the blurb....

> Set in the sinister atmosphere of a lonely island where three
> strangers meet in mysterious circumstances and are
> forced to re-evaluate their pasts......

He stuck it back on the shelf and continued his search, fingering his way along the line until he came to a second possibility, lifting it from its place.

'Rosie's Games' - it had a front cover illustration of a youngish, quite attractive woman wearing a wistful expression, lying in long grass. There was a huge half planet behind her as if the scene had been shot in proximity to Saturn or Jupiter. He turned to the back.

> *A woman receives imaginary letters from an estranged sister*
> *whose life has been torn asunder by greed and false promises.*
> *Written with tenderness and eye-catching detail.*

He snorted and stuffed it back in its rightful place on the shelf. He was getting nowhere. Next came 'Obsessions Of The Night' – a large breasted woman dominated the front cover, clasping her hands and looking longingly towards 'mountains' which featured as two equilateral triangles in the background. He turned to the blurb...

> *the intricate throes of obsession,*
> *coupled with deceit and double-dealings.*
> *A novel of love...of hate, of passion... despair ...*
> *and ultimately*
> *of great...great... hope!*

It was, it seemed, the final straw....He raised the book, shaking it vehemently, like some 'new-age' evangelist in the High Street.....
'Who fucking cares?'
He was looking directly at Gerald, as if holding him personally responsible for the book's publication.
'Who gives a shit?' His eye turned once more to the details printed on the back cover..... '*A haunting tale. The writer touches our emotions with the delicacy of a neuro-surgeon,......*Big fucking deal. Neuro-surgeons should be fixing people's fucking heads, not writing fucking books!'
Gerald reached for his Golden Virginia tin. The customer turned the book a few times in his hand as confirmation of its worthlessness, before returning it to its place on the shelf, after which, he continued his search.

After several further rejections he took hold of one which had a bare-breasted woman lying on a settee on the front cover. He gave it a quick perusal and took it to the counter.

'This'll do,' he said finally, though still with an air of some grievance as he reached into his pocket. Gerald popped the book in a bag and the money in the till. The man left the shop.

He had been his final customer and 'Hollywood Slappers Come Clean', his final sale.

At quarter to six exactly Gerald picked up his small bag and popped out to the back of the shop. He did a quick check and reappeared in the front, where he sorted a few things out before making his way down the aisle. As he did so he cast a look round at the shelves and stacks and opened the door to hear the familiar jingle. He turned the lights off and seconds later, the door was locked and he made his way across the road towards Sainsbury's.

He walked past the supermarket's huge low-level red brick building until he came to the end of the road, where he turned left and walked about forty yards.

He stopped and looked back. His shop – which had been his father's before him – was still visible – a small isolated block in the quickly fading light – the areas on each side having been derelict for some time.

He stood a little longer and then walked slowly up the street.

It was at about that moment that a small yellow and orange glow appeared in the rear of the shop. It began as faint illumination near the door, but spread quickly, taking in pretty much all that lay before it, until it reached the rear part of the shop itself. From then on it was easy pickings as it began to work its way relentlessly through the thousands of books and magazines, until some fifteen minutes or so later, the whole shop was a blazing inferno licking high into the night sky.

Gerald stood behind a small pillar and watched, as 'seemingly every word to have been presented in print' went up in flames in a matter of minutes.

It was a beautiful sight – the contorting, twisting patterns of scarlet, yellow and orange, set against the backdrop of a quickly-darkening sky.

In what appeared to be a matter of minutes, though was in reality, considerably longer, 'Gerald's Books' was little more than a shambles of black stone and ashes.

Soon, sirens and vividly oscillating patterns of blue joined the melee until the road by the shop was awash with fire-engines, flashing lights and police cars.

Gerald waited for a moment and then turned and made his way, head bowed up the street. He glanced again at his watch. Everything seemed to be in order. He'd followed the instructions to the last detail. He didn't look back again, he just continued walking up the street, assured that there'd be some money to be made from books after all.

Late Afternoon
in a Spanish Village

Celeste Warburton raised a foot a few inches on the balcony railing and glanced down at the mid-thigh to lower region of her leg. Late twenties or not, there was still – as she was often at pains to remind herself – much to admire in the mirror: a mid-coffee tan which would likely see her through July and August – buttocks and breasts both firm and prominent but without excess or wasted flab – eyes painstakingly crafted above a neat aquiline nose and lips tight and slightly curved. For some years she had worn her hair close – Mia Farrow style – a pair of oversized sunglasses completing the post-punk 'feature-ad' look.

She periodically turned her eyes to her husband – similarly reclined but naked except for a pair of boxer-shorts – noting that he too had left the dull pastiness of their homeland behind, even acquiring something of the suave sexiness of the young native Spaniards.

She forced herself to look away, turning instead to the low-lying hills to the north and to memories of the previous evening – the loss of a beautiful Spanish girl, whose father – the restaurant owner – had sadly taken exception to Celeste running her fingers through the twenty year old girl's waves of auburn hair and telling her she was 'beautiful'. He had been quite heated on the point, stabbing his finger repeatedly at a 'family photo' whilst telling her (Celeste that is) that such behaviour had no place on these shores. The girl herself had simply smiled. But for all that, it had seemed best not to pursue it, sensing the furore that would likely follow, not to mention the irrevocable rift in the family. This was Spain after all.

Her thoughts were interrupted by a burst of activity in the street below; a smattering of locals or whoever they were, gathering at the roadside, nestling small children in their folds or seating them at regular intervals in the shade of trees.

Her husband, Kenneth (Ken or 'K') was quickly out of his seat, pointing out that something appeared to be happening, something major by all accounts. His wife stirred herself sufficiently to peer briefly through a gap in the railing.

'Maybe someone's coming,' she said, resolved to resisting any attempt to interrupt her afternoon routine.

'Quite possibly,' said her husband, looking impishly across at his wife.

She eased a foot a few inches further up the balcony railing.

'Behave,' she said, smiling 'At least for now.'

About a hundred yards up the street a series of oblong tables had been placed at the roadside and covered with a white cloth. A number of helpers were busily arranging a number of accoutrements upon them. They appeared to be figurines, pots, jewellery, fabrics, and what seemed to be swords and pieces of armour. A small wicker casket was placed at the head of one of the tables, shrouded in a light cream cheesecloth.

From the top of the street a pastor, dressed in a magnificently ordained cloak of jewels that glistened and shimmered under the sun, made his way along the line of onlookers, distributing what appeared to be small tasselled artefacts and extended leaves bound by thin strips of twine. Having distributed his wares he returned to a table and joined the man in white flanked by the darker frocked vergers at each end.

On the balcony, Ken had struggled to his feet. He yawned and reached for his glass to pad in his flip-flops through the patio window into the bedroom and through to the kitchen at the back.

'Yes please.' As usual, her timing was impeccable – catching him just as he was about to disappear – glass in hand – over the threshold. He sighed and returned to snatch the glass from her raised hand.

'Thankyou darling,' she smiled, her head tilted coquettishly, her arm returning to the chair rest.

'Bit busy in the street,' he said, his voice drifting from behind kitchen blinds, accompanied by the chink of ice dropping in glasses.

She leant forward, reaching for the balcony rail, peering onto the activity below.

'Looks like some kind of religious thing,' she said, raising the sunglasses and speaking now entirely to herself.

Her husband placed the two sizzling glasses on the plastic table and stretched a hand to stifle a yawn.

Beneath them, the scene was set.

The event – a throwback to the ancient Moors, but with both Greek and Christian undertones – began with the visitation of an ancient cleric who made his way round the narrow bend at the end of the lane under the watchful eye of the spectators who responded by tossing tiny bunches of leaves tied with twine in his direction.

'Someone's coming,' said Ken, observing the crowd throwing small objects at a figure who seemed to have appeared from nowhere.

'So you keep saying,' said his wife, her fingers tapping repeatedly against the arm of the chair.

Her husband raised the glass to his lips.

The cleric had been joined by the pastor. The crowd – and Ken – watched as, in time-honoured tradition, the man knelt at the pastor's feet and pursed his lips against the lower folds of his smock. Ken took another drink and resumed his seat, raising his glass to eye the tiny diamonds glinting in the refractions of ice.

Celeste was watching her husband. She loved the sight of him at this time of day – the way the light fell across the curve of his shoulders, making him glisten like a freshly basted bird, the hairs on his legs quivering like an army of tiny spiders. And the way he reclined in the chair, secretly lording in the knowledge that he was coming under such close scrutiny.

Replacing her glass on the table, she stood as if to stretch her limbs, and stepping across, extended a hand over his shoulder, leaning to purse her lips against the lower flank of his neck.

On the street below, pastor and assistant had made their move – the former taking a position behind, and reaching a hand across the brow of a younger cleric who had adopted a kneeling position before him.

A hand strayed to first one shoulder, and then the other, settling finally on the dome of his head which remained bowed. As the pastor reached for a goblet of solid silver he looked up, raising it to eye level and tilting towards the crowd, revealing to all that the vessel was clean (reference to an incident in local folklore when a priest had been duped into believing an urn came direct from the palace of Alhambra, when in fact it was a mere pot of cheap metal forged by soldiers!)

Celeste's hand slipped across first one shoulder, and then the other, and then down her husband's chest, her fingers brushing lightly through the nests of hairs. When they were close to his waistband, she paused and knelt behind him to brush her lips against the nape of his neck – her fingers stirring round the upper reaches of his naval. For the moment he could do little but recline into her shoulder, aware only of the sensations of breath on his ear and the stirring of fingers round the rim of his shorts.

The pair entered the bedroom and eased the curtains to, allowing only the thinnest trace of sunlight to seep from the balcony onto the far wall. Within seconds Ken had taken his place, arranging himself crucifix-style on the bed. Minutes later, having secured his arms firmly at two of the corners, Celeste made her way to the bathroom, to emerge moments later and take a position by the door.

Back on the street the people had begun their slow procession past the pastor, observing the tiny ornaments and brooches – testaments to the Moorish devotion to intricate decoration and the Islamic reflection of 'unity' – each jostling for position alongside diamond-backed bracelets of the fifteenth century. And all without touching – touching was strictly prohibited.

Clad in tiny black panties and stockings and suspenders (purchased on a recent trip to Granada and hand-decorated with tiny gypsy-pearls and an elaborate array of sequins) his wife began rotating the intricate decoration and tiny patterns through the full three hundred and sixty degrees in a series of sensual swaying movements. Ken gazed in awe; she was beautiful. He had said it many times and would say it many times more, particularly when bound beneath her, his arms strapped to the two corners of the bed. Touching was – from necessity – strictly prohibited. Only *she* would be allowed to do the touching.

On the street below, the people could, if they wished, make their way across the road to kneel before the pastor to receive the 'blessing', a hand passed lightly from the left shoulder, over the head to the right shoulder – a re-enactment of an early tradition when the peasants were 'physically' cleansed in the presence of God.

Only when the time was right, did Celeste make her way slowly across the room and kneel down to straddle her husband – a hand passing lightly from one shoulder to the other – closely followed by lips, brushing gently against the moist brown skin.

Some moments later on the street below, having received their final blessing, the crowd parted for the raising of a huge cross and the climactic 'Catechism Of Light' – a hauntingly beautiful chant stemming from around 500 to 600 AD.

Whilst, in the room above, Ken finally got the green light to ejaculate into his wife – as fearsome and copious an emission as might be found anywhere in the village or indeed in the surrounding hillsides and olive groves.

And for a brief moment, the village was at one: a unified act of contrition that rose and hung in the air, and then eased and waned, before coming to an eventual standstill.

A final wave of the crowd – and gentle thrusting from Ken – completed the scene and for some moments the pair lay still, restoring their breath and spreading their legs idly across the thin duvet sheet.

It would be a while before either summoned the energy to raise themselves from the bed to make their way to the bathroom and the hot soothing jets of the shower. Ken led the way, his wife close at hand to join him on the porcelain, her face held high to the welcoming spray.

It was some time later, that the pair emerged once more onto the balcony with renewed glasses of gin and tonic foaming and bubbling round boulders of ice and thick slices of lemon. The stifling heat of the afternoon had relented, leaving a balmy warmth that brushed lazily against their freshened limbs.

They yawned and looked down to where spectators and clerics alike slowly dispersed to the flanks to drift off up the lane into small winding pathways and alleyways. The figures in the black robes and caps had remained at the table and were carefully wrapping and replacing the artefacts and treasures in a wooden box as two policeman looked on from a distance.

'They're strange aren't they, the Spanish, the way they carry on,' said Celeste, watching the scene and absently twirling the contents of her glass around the chunks of ice and lemon. 'Did you hear that peculiar wailing noise.'

'Mm...Maybe it's the heat,' said Ken, drinking deeply, savouring the rich aromatic tang of the gin.

'You see the guy on the right in the vicar's gear packing the souvenirs away,' he said, tilting his head vaguely in the direction of the tables. 'He looks a bit like the guy who threw a wobbly in the restaurant last night – remember.'

Celeste remembered, but said nothing. She tossed all of a quarter of the drink down her throat and flopped herself down on the reclining chair, where, once settled, she glanced down at the mid-thigh to lower region of her leg, reassured that it was well on its way to a 'mid-coffee' brown.

Looking Out For 648

The bus slowed to a halt for three people to board. The driver watched as an elderly woman found support from the door rail and hauled herself with some difficulty onto the deck. He told her it was okay and not to rush. Having secured her embarkation, she made a point of showing him her card – holding it up for a number of seconds – aware that card-carriers were expected to offer the card to the driver for inspection. He gave a quick nod and pressed the appropriate button on his machine.

She made her way slowly, leaning slightly forward in the manner of many people of more senior years. She took a seat on the left not far from the exit door. The seats between her and the front of the bus were mostly occupied.

A quite large woman cradling a straw shopping bag in her lap, sat back in one seat, or slightly more than one seat to be exact, glancing left and right out of the windows as if making mental notes of people passing by and anything else worth observing.

To her left, a thinner woman – older than the first, sat in a slightly sideways pose like a child caught in an old fashioned photograph. She held her handbag protectively in her lap as if its contents were her life's possessions or a small incendiary device.

In front of both of them, a third woman gave an impression of unease, pressing her left arm on the seat by her side as if for extra stability and endlessly glancing round.

Behind the woman with the shopping basket a ruddy complexioned man with a moon-round face and flat cap sat with his arms folded across his chest. Behind them the bus was empty.

The driver waited till his latest recruit was seated before pulling away. Occasional words were passed between one or two passengers, but apart from that they waited patiently and sat quietly for their turn to disembark.

The driver was a big-bodied guy, who filled his limited cabin space almost to the brim. You could imagine on hot sunny days, stuck in a traffic jam, he'd probably imagine life as a farmer or a steeplejack. Fortunately on this particular day, it wasn't excessively hot though the sun was out, and conditions weren't helped by a traffic jam, due to essential engineering-work being conducted over a two month period on piping under the road surface.

There was a sign about it, apologising in advance for inconvenience caused. The seriousness of the jam depended on the time of day. Early afternoon wasn't a particularly good time. Later in the afternoon was far worse. It was now two-thirty and the driver was expecting delays.

At the next stop a sole passenger boarded. He was an Asian male, or at least of Asian origin, possibly in his early twenties, carrying a small holdall in his left hand. Unusually for these times, he paid his fare in cash and then waited a moment, asking the driver if he knew where number 648 might be on Eastern Road. He was trying to get to 648 and thought it might be in the next half mile or so of the bus route. The driver sat back and frowned, giving it some thought. He took pride in knowing his route and liked to think he could recall most of its details as and when required.

'You're sure it's 648?' he said in a big booming voice, appropriate from one bearing such a large framed body. It was a voice that carried easily into the bus behind him - an advantage for communication with passengers whose validity to travel sometimes required further confirmation.

'Yes...648,' the man said, enunciating each number with clarity to avoid any possible confusion. He spoke with a strong Asian accent which made hearing a little difficult. As the bus pulled away there was a short silence as the driver continued to think where it might be and the passenger took a place on the flip-up seat by the window.

The other passengers took note of the new arrival as he eased the seat down and took his place directly opposite the largish woman with the straw shopping bag.

The woman opposite watched him with some interest – maybe because he was looking for a number 648, or possibly because he was Asian or of Asian origin. The driver was still trying to recall where, if anywhere, 648 was likely to be.

'It could be on the stretch passed the Vauxhall garage,' he said, his voice booming back into the main body of the bus. 'There's the supermarket, then you've got two blocks of flats before the shopping parade. It could be in the stretch after that. What exactly is it that you're looking for. Is it a shop or what?'

It was a little difficult for the man to hear the driver now as he had his back to him. He leant to his right slightly before speaking.

'It's 648,' he repeated, 'It was the only number I was given.'

'And you don't know anymore, or any streets that might be nearby,' said the driver, half his mind on the road and the other half trying to identify the numbers they were passing. The traffic was slowing now as they approached the stationary line of traffic before the engineering works.

'Cos if you had the name or some details it might be easier to figure out where it is your looking for.'

'It's 648,' repeated the man, returning his gaze to his front, smiling at the woman opposite, who was still scrutinising him closely, the straw shopping bag nestling in her lap. The woman in front glanced uneasily at the surroundings, maybe of a mind to see if she could throw any light on its whereabouts. The first woman took it upon herself to explain the driver's difficulty.

'If you had some more details of the place, then it might be easier for the driver to be able to tell you where it might be so's you'd know where to get off the bus you see,' she said, speaking forcefully, but – as she saw it – patiently, with him being Asian and to ensure he understood the driver's predicament. The man continued to smile, nestling the small holdall on his lap.

The bus came to a standstill and would remain in its place in the queue for some time, due to the engineering works. The driver offered an apology and an explanation for the delay, telling them about the works they were carrying out under the road. The moon-faced man remarked that it was a pity they had to be doing it in the middle of the afternoon and there was some agreement, but the thing is when would be a 'good' time for doing the work?

'Normally it's about a ten minute wait,' explained the driver,' but we *are* moving, slowly.'

The passengers stared at the line of shops and flats and the long thin hedgerow running the length of the dual-carriageway, and rapidly wearying from its countless years of exhaust fumes.

'Are you're sure that the place you're looking for is on this part of Eastern Road?' asked the driver, looking up to the mirror that reflected down the aisle.

'Because this road's a very long road that stretches back before the roundabout – almost back as far as Walthamstow. It may be that the place you're looking for is somewhere back before the roundabout.'

The man smiled and turned in his seat mumbling something inaudible to the others. 'We can't be sure that it's in this part of the road that we're on now,' continued the driver. 'It might be on the way back towards Wanstead or towards Leytonstone even. It may be that the numbers are different back there,' he explained. 'Back Leytonstone way there's rows of shops and businesses, same as along here – it may be one of them,' he said, looking hopefully through the right-hand window.

'Over the Leytonstone part they got some new businesses just opening,' said the moon-faced man. 'It was in the local papers last week. They had to postpone the building 'cause there was some trouble over the planning details. Some firm reckoned they hadn't got proper planning permission or something and they couldn't complete the building unless that was sorted.'

'Well you get a lot of trouble over a lot of these places nowadays,' said the driver looking up into his mirror. 'Whether it's all above-board and on the level. Cos the authorities have got to know who it is whose got the rights – cos sometimes the leases or the deeds or the freeholds or whatever it is, can cause a lot of problems.'

The man continued to sit patiently, clutching his holdall and smiling at the woman opposite, who in her turn, maintained her own vigilant watch on proceedings. She repeated the driver's point just in case he hadn't fully grasped it.

'Maybe the place you're looking for is on a different part of the road and maybe it's back Walthamstow way,' she said, speaking particularly loudly and even more clearly.

The man smiled.

'It's all to do with the law,' the moon-faced man said, staring ahead as the others looked casually around them. 'But it can get very complicated.'

'One of the new buildings Walthamstow way collapsed before it was ready and finished,' said the woman on the left. 'They was talking about it on the news. Fortunately there was no-one in it at the time, or there could have been people killed. The council was looking into it to find out who was responsible. They had to start the building all over again,' she said, clutching her handbag and staring at the passing cars.

'Well that can happen a lot these days with some of these building firms,' said the driver, looking to his mirror. 'Half the time you can't be sure exactly who it is you're dealing with – there's a guy or maybe a firm who gets the contract and he sub-contracts and of course he's looking for the guy whose going to do it for the least cost so he can save himself money - he wants to get the job done as cheap as he can, but half the time he don't know exactly who it is he's sub-contracting to. And if it's one of these foreign firms, you don't know whether they're bona-fides or what, but they can still set themselves up as a building firm. I mean I'm not saying anything about them being foreign or nothing like that. I don't mean it like that. I mean a lot of them are probably bona-fides, but you can't be sure – that's all I'm saying. And the guy who'se got the contract, he's only gonna spend as little as he can get away with - cos it's all down to money in the end.'

'Yeh well everything comes down to money these days,' said the woman with the shopping basket. The woman in front nodded and switched her gaze nervously to the side.

'They say that money talks and they're right,' put in the moon-faced man, arms folded emphatically across his chest.

The driver looked again to his mirror, as if seeking contact with the man, despite him being out of vision behind the stairs.

'If you haven't been there before and don't know much about it, it may be that your 648 don't even exist anymore,' said the driver, 'or it may have been taken over by some other firm by now.'

The Asian man smiled, and nursed the holdall, seemingly unconcerned at either possibility, convinced that 648 would be out there somewhere.

There was a sudden slowing in the traffic and they continued to crawl for some fifty yards or so before coming to another standstill.

For a few moments silence prevailed as eyes peered out at yet more roadside shops, a car show room and a pub. The man perused the buildings with interest. If his destination happened to be in the vicinity, he didn't want to miss it. A voice broke the silence.

'Well I'm getting off at the hospital and that's about a mile or so. And there isn't much beyond that. So I doubt if the place you're looking for is much further up,' said the woman with the shopping bag, ostensibly directing her comment at the man, though offering it as general information to everyone as far as the driver.

'So you don't know whether it's a shop or what then,' said the driver, looking up into his mirror.

'It's a small place – 648,' said the man.

'A small place. So it's a small place you're looking for – but a small 'what', we don't know - Well that might make it even more difficult,' said the driver, looking to the side out of his window.

'You don't know what kind of a place,' said the woman with the shopping bag, as the bus rolled back into motion for thirty or forty yards.

'I only have a number...648,' the man said again.

'Yes well we know that,' she said, turning to the window, seeming to share a little of the driver's frustration.

'There's lots of flats above shops along here,' said the moon-faced man, 'If it's along here, it's more than likely going to be a shop or a flat above a shop.'

'I think if I was you I'd get off the bus, have a closer look and maybe ask someone at one of the shops along here.' said the driver looking up into his mirror. 'You never know, someone might be able to point you more in the direction. Cos as I say it could be back behind the roundabout, it could even be Wanstead way, or even back towards Walthamstow. Cos we're moving again now – it was the engineering works causing the hold-up. So I reckon your best bet'd be to get off at the next stop and take it from there. And if you want to get back to Wanstead you could get the same bus or you could change at at the roundabout for a 203, or you can get a 161– that'll take you all the way back to Wanstead. For Leytonstone, you'll have to change – probably at Wanstead. You can get a 224 from there, or you could get a 177, but it goes a slightly different route and takes a little longer.'

The passengers sat quietly, looking to the front or out at the passing pavement.

The man sat too, nursing his holdall in his lap and staring passively out of the window. After a few moments he turned in his seat and leaned to press the button at the side of the aisle. As the bell rang the driver's eye returned to his mirror.

With the slowing of the bus the man eased himself off the seat and stood up. The bus came to a halt and the rear doors opened automatically. Clutching his holdall under his arm, the man held the supporting rail with his right hand and looked around smiling.

'Well I hope you find it,' said the woman with the shopping bag. 'You'll probably find it back somewhere before the roundabout,' said the moon-faced man.

The woman in front turned nervously, supporting herself with her arm against the seat.

He stepped down off the bus, paused for a second and began walking alongside the bus as the doors closed and it began to pull away.

The woman nursed her shopping bag on her lap and the moon-faced man sat with his arms folded against his chest and the woman in front leant into the seat and glanced nervously around her.

The driver shuffled in his seat. It was beginning to get a bit warm in the cabin, particularly after being stuck in the queue. There were times when he wished he was a farmer.

'Never really said what it was he was looking for,' said the woman with the shopping basket. 'He didn't seem to know much about it.'

'All he had was a number and that's about all,' said the moon-faced man. 'I don't reckon it's round here though.'

'No I think you're right. Probably further back, maybe more towards Wanstead way,' said the woman.

'Unless it's even further back,' said the driver, looking in his mirror. 'Could be it's even somewhere back towards Walthamstow,' he said.

The bus drew to a halt at the next bus stop and waited a few moments for the elderly woman to disembark. The driver watched as she found support from the hand rail and eased herself down with some difficulty. He told her to take her time and not to rush. When she had safely disembarked the doors closed and the bus continued its journey.

* * * * *

Somewhere in Arkansas

Lenny's Place was a small place somewhere at the side of the highway that drifted its way across the flatlands heading over in the direction of Fort Smith. Lenny had been out back of the bar a while trying to clear a couple of cloths that had somehow stuck themselves round the grating to the drain. He cursed and stretched a hand, finally extracting the offending mess and flinging it into a sluice bucket by the ladders against the wall. Wiping thick oily streaks across his brow and eyes, he raised his six foot two frame and dragged himself towards the rear door, pulling his hat more firmly round the rim of his forehead before making his way through the kitchen door, past the cooling shelf to the bar area.

The bar itself was a long low-lit tunnel of oakwood.

Lenny ambled round the corner of the shelving and made a grab for a bottle of water from the cool shelf, simultaneously flicking the plastic seal into the nearby trash can.

Seated round the other side of the bar was a man, his upper torso curled over the bar surface leaning on his elbows. His face remained more or less hidden by a broad black hat pulled low as if to dissuade any attempt at closer identification. He wore a large flapping opened collar shirt and black trousers and a neckerchief looped round his veiny neck. To his right a beer lay largely ignored and to his left, a packet of Marlborough, the contents of which were reduced about every ten minutes. Lines of sweat had been coursing round his ears and collecting in his collar for most of the day. He occasionally made a gesture of removing their excess but mostly found it too much of an effort. He raised his beer and brushed his hat back a fraction.

As Lenny finished the water and chucked the empty plastic in the trash can, a shadow appeared in the doorway behind them.

It stopped a few seconds and wiped a hand across its brow. Lenny glanced towards the door. The man at the bar reached for a Marlborough and stared at the whiskey bottles

The shadow remained some moments longer, then ventured into the gloom and made his way towards the bar, dumping a string-tied burlap sack at his side. Lenny gave him a quick nod and popped a crumpled cloth on the corner of the shelf. The first man lit the Marlboro, releasing the smoke in soft plumes in the direction of the whiskey bottles. The newcomer took his place some four or five feet at his side and manoeuvred the stool into position. He nodded in the man's direction and then at Lenny.

'I'll have a beer,' he said flatly, drawing his feet onto the foot-rail and removing a line of wet grease that had gathered in the line of his collar. Lenny pulled the tap and placed the *Miller* in front of him. The newcomer dragged the hand across his forehead, sighed and reached for the glass.

'Hotter 'n a bitch in a burning barn out there,' he confirmed, smacking his lips and replacing the glass on the bar top. The first man drew from the cigarette.

'Get's so you can't be thinking o' nothing' but sittin' around for a little breeze to come along.'

He had a thin, drawn face dominated by a drooping tash lining either side of his mouth like a couple of squirrel tails. He wore a hat, the brim of which drooped and sank hiding most of the top side of his head. Thin rivers of sweat trickled a path from his forehead down his cheeks to nestle irritatingly in the bristles. He twitched to ease them away and reached again for his glass.

'Been over pickin' up some work Van Buren way couple o' months. Hotter 'n a bitch on heat over those parts. Glad just to get my money and get me 'board the next freight train. Guy needs a break when it's hotter 'n a racoon in a rat hole.'

'Ain't gonna change none,' said Lenny, resuming the wiping next to a line of glasses. He levelled his eyes toward the bowed head of the stranger. 'You from these parts?'

'No sir, just passing through.' The man paused to examine his beer-glass and cast a quick glance at the figure to his left. 'Got a wind of work going down over some o' them loggin' ranges and made my way down from a little place called Hela Springs.'

Lenny took the cloth and gave it a few squeezes over the sink. The first man drew on the cigarette and eased the plumes into the gloom beyond the till.

'Come from Oklahoma originally,' said the visitor. 'Dustbowl country. My father and his before him. Had to git out when the old dust storms come sweeping cross the land like a tornado in a broom cupboard. Sure in hell was a bitch.'

He chuckled and reached for his beer. Lenny reached down to wipe some residue from a lower shelf. The first man flicked a head of ash into the tin tray on the bar.

'Found ourselves out California way – orange country – land o' milk 'n honey so they reckoned. I don't have much recollections o' no honey and wan't much by way o' milk either by all accounts.'

He drew a hand across his brow and then raised the glass to his lips. Lenny straightened a line of glasses and turned to take a bunch of cubes from the ice-box.

'Ain't never been California way,' said Lenny. 'Was in Little Rock and Hot Springs back one summer. Hotter 'n hell down those parts.'

The man turned his glass pensively. 'Ain't no big deal,' he said flatly. 'I grew up in a town just off the ninety nine 'tween Fresno and Sierra Nevada. One borin' place; pickin' beans all day 'n shakin' hands with coyotes every which way.'

'Gimme a whiskey,' said the first man slipping the beer glass along the bar.

'Water?' Lenny reached up for the bottle and removed the top. 'Uh uh.'

'Whiskey man huh?' The second man watched the thick fluid spilling into the glass and flicked his hat above the band of sweat.

'Was working the log-ranges Tennessee way few summers ago. Guys there – hitched their own little racket round back o' the loadin' area; hootch swimmin' round the glass thick as boot polish, got a kick like a mule in a candy store.' He took a wistful look at the drink and downed it with a swift flick of the wrist. The man raised the glass to his lips. Lenny finished with the ice box and quickly secured the lid before the heat got to creeping its way into the cubes.

'I'll take another beer,' said the visitor, pushing the glass to one side and reaching for a small cloth stuck in his right hand pocket. 'What they call ya?'

'Lenny.' Lenny held the tilted glass under the tap and wiped the top foam with a knife. He placed the glass and whipped the beer-mat away in preference for a replacement that wasn't soaked through.

'Joe,' said the man, extending a hand which Lenny reached for as a matter of courtesy. 'California ain't no big deal,' he said. 'Hotter 'n a bitch in hell round those desert areas; Death Valley's a real shit. Ain't no surprise how it come to get its name. Hunderd ten and more summer time. No way a guy needs hundred ten crawlin' its way up his ass,' said Joe. 'Was over San Jose way couple o' summers ago. Eighty in the shade. Met a gal been working the bars in San Luis. Singin' gal; could bang a tune out with her head stuck deep in a corn sack.'

The man tossed the remainder of his drink down his throat with a quick flick of the wrist and handed the glass to Lenny.

'Make her a large one,' he said, holding the glass in front of Lenny's face.

'Make it two,' said Joe, looking on and quickly draining the remaining droplets of beer. Lenny poured the drinks and eased the glasses down the bar in opposite directions. 'California ain't no big deal,' said Joe, holding the glass at eye level against the shelf light and easing it gently from side to side.

He replaced the glass on the counter and leant forward lightly on his lower arms. 'Trouble there nowadays is too many o' these college-types fussin' every which way. Get's so a guy can't think straight.' A tongue clicked pensively against the roof of his mouth..... 'Take black guys – or niggers.'

For a moment the glass appeared to hover in mid-air. He turned swiftly.

'Now don't get me wrong....It ain't got nothin' 'gainst a guy bein' black. Ain't nothin' to do with bein' no racialist!.....But that's what they used to call 'em...'nigres'; that was the word they used. And I hear some of 'em calling themselves that now – some o' these young 'ns. It don't mean nothin' – on'y words...That's all I'm sayin'...'

He hunched a shoulder, lowering the glass to the counter. 'But I ain't got no problem with that. That's what a guy wants, that's okay with me. That's his business.' He took a slug of whisky. "s on'y words...' he said.

Lenny leant against the bar and took a final drink from the water bottle. The first man drew quietly on his Marlborough. 'Gimme another shot,' said the first man, his voice growing edgy in the late afternoon heat. He switched his gaze from the bottles to Lenny. 'And make it a water too.'

'Double it,' said Joe, switching his gaze to the bottles and then to Lenny.

As Lenny took the bottle and was in the process of spilling generous measures in the two glasses, a second figure appeared in the doorway and stood momentarily observing the scene.

Lenny glanced over his shoulder. Joe turned an eye to his left and the first man held his eye on the till.

The figure ventured from the silhouette of the doorway to make his way to the bar. He took a standing place between the men and popped a worn canvas holdall at his feet. He was a negro. Maybe six, six foot two. He wore a thin vest that clung in tight strands to his oily torso, displaying two thick arms, the muscles heavy and strong.

Lenny nodded in his direction. The man returned the nod. Joe took the water and half drained the glass.

'Gimme a beer,' said the man leaning casually against the bar and tilting his hat to a point where it seemed ready to topple from his head. Lenny pulled the tap and placed the beer before him.

'Passin' through?' asked Lenny.

'Kind o'.' The man raised the glass to his lips. 'Doin' a bit of labouring just up the road at the site just before the highway. New mall. Shoppin' place. Hotter 'n shit in this sun.' Both men nodded. Joe extended an arm.

'Joe,' he said, by way of simple announcement. The man acknowledged the hand.

'Denny,' he said, reaching for the beer glass. Joe chuckled and nodded in the direction of Lenny.

'I like that,' he said. 'We got Denny. And the barman's Lenny. Lenny and Denny. You should open up a burger joint at Coney Island with a handle like that.'

Lenny made his way to the sink and ran the tap. He took a flannel and doused it under the warm stream and then bathed the sloppy material over his brow and forehead.

'How long ya figuring on stickin' on the project?' he asked raising the water bottle to his lips and drinking deeply. Denny shrugged.

'Couple o' months, could be more. Gonna see how things break when they start laying the bricks. Helluva job when you got the sun bakin' it dry every foot yer tryin' to dig.'

'What's it yer building' then?' asked Joe.

'Shoppin' mall and couple o' stores or summin' Ain't too sure exactly what it is they're planning. I'll be around most likely while they're layin' the bricks and then get back homeward bound once winter starts showin' its face.'

'Where you from?' asked Lenny, sliding his way over to the chips packets on a card pinned to one of the bar's stanchions.

'Alabama.' Denny raised the glass and quickly lowered it, his eyes fixed on the rapidly moistening beer-mat beneath. Lenny looked over at the man's bowed head.

'Much work Alabama way?' he asked.

'"pends,' said the man, turning the beer-mat in tiny spirals with the glass.

'Was working the paper works round Mobile way and done some peach and water-melon pickin' down the plains for couple o' years.'

Joe raised his glass, drank and wiped his lips with his cuffs.

Behind them the late afternoon sunlight drifted along the bar tables – the only movement, the occasional raising of a glass to lips. Lenny was half way to picturing a bar down a Colorado ski-slope with an iced cola waiting on a table, as Joe tipped the whiskey and turned to his left.

'Guess it ain't always been a stroll in the park for you guys down Alabama way,' he said, popping the glass back and holding his eye on Denny.

Lenny's eye raised a fraction and the first man switched his gaze temporarily to his right. Denny fingered his glass and stared at the counter.

'Hear tales 'bout the police kicking the shit out o' y'all back there in the old days, get's a guy thinkin',' he added, smacking his lips wistfully and turning the glass repeatedly in his hand.

'Yeh well it ain't too bad now,' said Denny, raising his glass and holding his gaze on the bar. Joe looked up.

'I gotta question,' he said, in the tone of one set to embark on important business. He placed his glass on the mat and looked Denny in the eye.

Lenny had taken a cloth and was busily rotating it on the inside of a glass.

'Don't take this wrong fella, but we was talking' earlier____ '

'*You* was talking earlier,' interjected Lenny quickly.

'Yeh…well. I gotta question.' He stopped a moment allowing the question to form clearly in his mind.

'You get sore if you get to be called a nigger 'stead o' just a black man?'

Lenny stiffened and reached for the next glass. The first man turned to his right. Denny remained head-bowed, gazing down at the bar top. He drank slowly and then turned casually to Joe. 'Usually find my name works fine,' he said simply. 'Long as a person knows it.' He raised his glass to his mouth.

Joe thought for a moment.

'Yeh, but what I'm sayin' is...Let's say you're in this shoppin' mall you're building, buyin' some stuff and there's some kid sniffin' round your ankles. And the mother calls to the kid. Should it be 'get out of the way of the black man' 'stead of 'get out of the way of the nigger' or what?'

The question received a few seconds contemplation. The first man eyed Joe carefully. Denny stared for some moments into the glass he was holding in his right hand.

'How about 'just get outta the *guy's* way,' he said, looking at Joe. Joe turned the answer over in his mind. The guy didn't seem to be getting his point.

'Yeh but what I'm sayin' is_____'

'Leave it fella.'

The interruption came from the left where the man was looking long and hard in Joe's direction. Joe looked up and raised a hand.

'Hey, there ain't no problem; I ain't meanin' nothin'.'

'You heard the guy.'

'Yeh....but he ain't answered the question.'

'Or maybe you ain't hearin' the answer.'

Lenny was watching Joe from his position by the potato chips. Denny stood leaning into the counter, nursing the glass lightly in the fingers of his right hand.

'I think I just heard the bell ringing for work to get started on those loggin' ranges you're headin' for,' said the first man, raising the whiskey to his lips, his eyes fixed firmly on the glass. Joe sat for a moment, gazing at the shelf across the bar, then he reached into his pocket and withdrew a small tumble of coins which he placed onto the counter. He stood and brushed his hat lazily against his side.

He stared through the doorway and made his way across the floor toward the shimmering sun, giving the man a wide berth in the process. Once in the doorway, he stood a moment in silhouette and replaced his hat firmly on his head.

'Guess I'll be gettin' along. Guy get's itchy stickin' round a place too long.' He hitched the burlap sack onto his right shoulder.

'Get's so a guy can't say nothin' these days,' he said, and then turned and disappeared from sight.

The first man had his eyes fixed firmly on the wall ahead. He turned and held the glass in Lenny's direction.

'Fill her up.'

Lenny took the glass and reached for the bottle and then looked across at Denny.

'Another beer?' he asked. Denny nodded and withdrew his eye from the empty doorway.

'Sorry 'bout that,' said Lenny, popping the beer in the space before him. 'On the house.' Denny shrugged and raised the glass.

"s okay. He maybe didn't mean nothin',' he said.

'Seems maybe the guy just likes to talk a little too much,' Lenny concluded, placing the beer on the counter.

'Seems so,' said the first man, reaching for a Marlborough.

Sunny Afternoon in Hamburg

He liked to stalk the waterfront like a rifleman – his camera constantly on the lookout. And as he peered over the railings to where the semi-diffused sunlight merged to a silvery blaze reflecting off the water, he thought he might have got something. He moved closer, his eyes narrowing to a tight squint – taking in the heavy cargo work of the estuary – huge ship-holdings lined against a backdrop of stacked containers and interwoven cranes, criss-crossing the sky in a wave of metallic patterns.

He got the long lens and checked the speed. He'd get a few shots. No problem with light. With luck, he'd get that eerie, ghostly effect; the boats and cranes punched huge in the frame.

He took a few shots and was immediately drawn to the jetty beneath, where people loitered or gave an impression of loitering: Lowry-type silhouettes, gazing into space, waiting to be caught while the going was good. Leaning on the railing for stability, he took three or four shots. And made a quick decision to move on.

Above, two U-Bahns rattled along the loop of elevated rail looking down on a small garden of trees, in the midst of which, about fifty yards from the promenade, and standing in virtual isolation, was a small imbiss – a kind of 'stand up' café selling hot and soft drinks and snacks. He'd grab a coffee and water there.

As he approached he couldn't help but notice the Coca Cola insignias blasted across every inch of available space – the canopies, the sun shields, the signs on the wall. And amongst it all – a lone customer, a young woman standing in profile at one of the tables.

He approached nonchalantly, camera in hand. It'd make an interesting shot – a young woman – alone – surrounded by the ultimate icon of American capitalism. But he knew the need to exert a little caution; there are those who take exception to being your 'art' and are inclined to confront you on the issue. His approach – a tried and trusted one by now – was to get himself settled a few yards away and give the impression that there may be a fault with the camera or something in need of checking – raising it to his eye and passing it across the scene until it just happens to frame his shot, at which point he would quickly take the picture and then continue to look through the viewfinder in a vague pretence of still checking it out.

As usual, it worked fine – she barely seemed to have noticed.

Picture secured, he replaced his camera, grabbed himself a coffee from the counter and took his place two tables away.

She was mid twenties perhaps, long dark hair, tee-shirt and casual jeans. He stole a few glances as he sipped his water. She occasionally stole a few glances back. He took out his U-Bahn map to check his next port of call. Possibly St. Pauli – or maybe one of the lakes.

He was in the process of deciding which, when he was aware of her approaching him. He wondered if he was about to be challenged about invading her privacy and impinging on her rights, but instead she smiled and asked if she could take a photo of him. He felt bolstered at the opportunity to show off a bit of his German.

'Ja, warum nicht?' It sounded impressive. He pointed out the simple automatic feature and allowed her to take the camera and frame him. Had she moved too far away he would have intervened, but she hardly seemed the type to run off with your camera. He attempted a smile and saw the opportunity to show off a bit more of his German.

'Darf ich ein Bild von Ihnen machen?' She smiled and he took the snap that he didn't really want, but it was all part of the ritual.

She expressed interest in the camera. But her observations quickly lost him and the pair promptly resorted to English which – as in the case of nearly every German he'd met under the age of about forty – was far better than his German anyway – the price you pay for attempting to avoid being the stereotyped 'Englishman abroad'.

He pointed out its relatively straightforward features – just the latest off the Canon SLR line. She weighed it and played with it a while, commenting on how light it was. He explained the advantage in taking his kind of pictures.

'And what kind of pictures are they?' she asked, appearing to be genuinely interested. He explained it was anything that grabbed his eye, sometimes people, quite often not. He took another drink. The coffee wasn't too bad – not too bitter and served hot, which wasn't always the case in these places.

Another train rattled its way above them, reminding him of his intent to move on soon. She turned her head to share the commotion as it passed by and then continued to sip at her beaker of mineral water. She had moved to the adjacent table and showed no intention of returning to her former spot.

There was that moment of each waiting for the other to speak.

'Do you live in Hamburg?' he asked.

She fingered the carton and looked across.

'Yes....I work not far from here and where I live is about ten minutes ride on the train.' Her English was excellent – typical Germanic precision, with its clear enunciation of consonants, making his attempts to converse in her own tongue seem even more feeble.

'Have you seen much of Hamburg?' she asked, the short 'a' sound ringing its almost received-pronunciation.

'A bit...but I'm not really into viewing places. I prefer just wandering round with my camera – the streets, railway stations, places like that.'

She tossed a shoulder-length mane of hair and turned to where a large boat, possibly a liner, crawling its way down its central channel, appeared to have come to a standstill.

'I like to come down here and walk along the waterfront, looking at the boats, particularly the larger ones, and imagine where they've come from or where they're going to. All those huge distances and far-off places; and yet moving so slowly, with all the time in the world.'

He followed her gaze, squinting into the piercing sunlight, the vessel – an indistinct grey shape standing in mid-water.

'You could have come from England I think in a boat,' she said, turning to face him. 'I think that's where they arrive and depart from – the landing point just over there.' She held her arm out, indicating the jetty some distance down the path.

'Mm.....takes a while though – about a day and a half I think,' he said.

She stirred the plastic cup between forefinger and thumb.

'Don't you think that's the way we should travel? A day and a half or even a week and a half.' She raised the cup and took another sip.

'Where are you heading next?' she asked.

'What, now or when I leave Hamburg?'

'Now, when you leave here. What are your plans?'

'Don't know, I might head off to St. Pauli,' he said.

'There's always the Reeperbahn. You know the Reeperbahn with the sex trade.'

He knew it well. He'd been there a few times – browsed through a few of the shops.

She was watching him closely, checking for a reaction. He knew the sex trade was different here – it being a port and everything. There was an openness, air of celebration even; something you'd never get in England, that's for sure.

'Prostitution is tightly controlled in Hamburg,' she said, gazing out across the water, her enunciation clear and precise.

She turned as another train looped its way above their heads, the tiny heads framed like punctuation-marks inside the oblong shapes of windows.

'I like the U Bahn or the S Bahn,' he said, 'Just sitting, riding around with no particular destination or intention in mind.'

They watched the tail of the train wind its final loop before disappearing from sight.

'Do you meet many people when you are wandering round on your own?' she asked.

'Not really, I tend to keep to myself. Occasionally get into a conversation in a pub, but mostly I just stay on my own and read.'

'So when you leave from here you will find a quiet place and then you can be on your own.'

'Not necessarily. Maybe....maybe not.'

She looked down at the table-top. 'I like to be on my own, but I have to like people too. Sometimes,' she said, finishing her drink and taking a few paces to throw the carton into a nearby dispenser.

'And how do you feel about being approached by strangers in the afternoons?' she asked, returning to her now adopted place at the next table.

'Okay....no problem,' he replied.

She looked across the narrow stretch that separated the water-front area from the buildings lining the street.

'I work in St. Pauli – not far from the area you're heading,' she continued. 'It's a pity that you can't understand more German because there are many nice bookshops with books that I think you would be interested in. There are some in English, but not many,' she said.

'I wouldn't expect it,' he replied. 'Try looking in English bookshops for books in German.'

There was a short silence. The boat in the estuary had barely moved.

She looked around the tables. 'Since I've been standing here no-one else has come. We talk and yet we are strangers. You are perhaps wishing you hadn't come here.' She smiled.

'Why should I think that? No-one forces me to stay here,' he said.

She turned to where the diamond reflections bounced off the canopy of the U-Bahn station. And then looked at her watch and reached down for her bag – her attention drawn to it as if looking for something.

He finished his coffee and followed her example of depositing the carton in the appropriate receptacle before returning to his table.

She had found what she was looking for. It was a small card which she held in the tips of her fingers. She looked at him when he returned to the table, and then handed it to him.

'I have my details here on this card,' she said. 'The address is a street off the Reeperbahn. You can come and see me at this address if you like. I would like it if you did. It's my daytime and early evening address you understand. I'm there until about ten o clock, except Tuesday.'

She quickly closed her bag and began to move away, stopping just briefly.

'It was nice to talk to you...and you letting me talk to you. And if you'd have asked me about taking a picture when you first got here it would have been alright,' she added with a smile. 'I have no problem about being photographed. My price is very reasonable.'

She turned and walked in the direction of the road by the U-Bahn station.

He read the card and popped it in his wallet.

Then he reached for his camera-bag and made his departure, quickening his pace as the next U Bahn train came into vision.

('U Bahn' - Equivalent of London's tube – though largely overground)

The Balcony Scene

Patrick and Norma McNeice stood together at the edge of the balcony of their beautifully appointed villa in the shadow of the Blue Ridge Mountains. His left hand clutched a glass of concentrated mango juice; for her it was apricot juice – rich and almost creamy in the dimpled glass. They gazed out over the peaks of the surrounding mountains; their dark grey shapes twisting and contorting, seeming – against the backdrop of bright sun and clear blue sky – like some devilish configurations emanating from the very jaws of hell.

Patrick and Norma were very much in love, and always had been, even back in their childhood days, when, rather than play with the other children on the swings and amongst the apple trees, they would drift down to the local stream together and hold hands, whisper sweet thoughts and playfully splash each other from the tiny pools that settled in the midst of the moss-strewn rocks. They would arrange for each other to be invited to tea and delight in catching each others' eye over anchovy soldiers and blueberry muffins.

Their schooldays had been wonderful times. Though neither had excelled in their studies nor displayed any particular prowess on the sports field, they had each other and would regularly and without embarrassment, indulge in brief kisses and gentle arm-stroking between classes and in the locker room after afternoon classes.

Marriage of course followed as naturally as light follows day, and the happy day occurred, in the eyes of the Lord, one May afternoon in the height of Spring. It had been a wonderful day;

the weather had been kind with a soft breeze blowing from the
east and they'd celebrated their union with a full-blown family
extravaganza under a canvass marquee. They felt no need for a
honeymoon, content as they were to allow themselves time
together in their wonderful mountainside villa at a tiny small-
holding amongst the Blue Ridge Mountains. They had delighted
in each others' and God's company, and for two wonderful
weeks, loved nothing more than to take long hikes across the
crags and slopes of the lower hills and to sit by the lakeside and
pray.

They'd given some thought to matters 'physical' and agreed
that simple touching and kissing were spiritual as much as
physical; a spirit of togetherness expressed through simple tactile
communication. Intercourse was of course for procreation, so
that would wait a while.

Everything was ticking along fine and they seemed to be
destined for a long and happy life together, had it not been for
the previous Saturday.

The day had begun the same as any other Saturday with a
morning prayer, a mango and apricot breakfast, weekly
shopping at the local mall and a bright and breezy walk to a
favourite spot of theirs, some quarter of a mile or so from their
home.

It was at about one-o-clock in the afternoon that the
doorbell rang and Norma, on answering the door, found one
of their neighbours – a new neighbour – on the doorstep
inviting the pair of them to a little party they were throwing
that night as a kind of 'Hi' to everyone in the neighbourhood.
It would be an open-house type arrangement: a free mixing of
souls and spirits – an ideal opportunity for getting to know
each other.

There was some hesitation from Norma who wasn't sure
where they stood on such matters. She excused herself for a
moment and went to discuss it with her husband. Rather than
hanging around waiting for the verdict, the neighbour

repeated the invite and left them with a small card bearing all the relevant details. The pair discussed the proposition and Patrick suggested that maybe it would be a good idea to accept the invitation, for they were, after all, part of a community and there was no reason for them to ignore everyone just because they had faith. He reminded her of when they had been little and tended to avoid other children and had got themselves a bit of a reputation for being standoffish and rude. Such qualities could easily be construed as sinful and perhaps they ought to be wary of keeping themselves to themselves too much. That settled the matter, for there was no way they could consider doing anything that might be seen as sinful. They would go to the party and be friendly and convivial and maybe even – you never know – enjoy themselves.

They took some time preparing themselves for the evening, for it was very rare for them to leave their home for any purpose other than shopping, to go to work, church, or to take a brisk walk amongst the surrounding hillsides. They wanted to look smart of course, but not ostentatious nor in any way excessively flamboyant or flashy. They knew it was customary to take a bottle of drink on such occasions and they left the house with a fine bottle of mango juice and a bottle of apricot conserve. The idea of taking anything alcoholic was clearly unthinkable.

They felt a little nervous as they approached the house, for they weren't at all sure what to expect, never having been to a party before and never having met any of the people who lived in their neighbourhood. But, after the rather awkward introductions, pleasantries and run-of-the-mill platitudes, the evening progressed, and things seemed to be going just fine. Everyone seemed to be mixing and milling around freely, without care of age or disposition, and in quite close proximity too, which was nice. They enjoyed chatting convivially with a few of their neighbours and enjoyed the mango and the apricot conserve, though as the evening wore on, they did begin to tire a little of the taste, not least because they were the only people drinking it. So later on when a young couple they'd been chatting with for some time who'd recently moved to the area from Baltimore, asked if they'd care to try a drink that they'd prepared themselves with 'their own fair hands', they jumped at the chance, having been reassured of course that it was totally alcohol free.

It seemed the couple specialised in exotic-style drinks but couldn't produce the kind of quantities that would give everyone at a party such as this, the chance to try them. On arrival, they had taken the drink upstairs to a 'special room' where it wouldn't be discovered by all and sundry. They had only been able to rustle up one bottle and were rather anxious not to have it discovered by some 'stranger' who might whip the bottle away to keep for themselves. Patrick and Norma quite understood this, particularly as the drink had taken so much time and trouble to prepare.

No-one seemed to mind, or even notice, as they followed the couple up the stairs to the landing which led to a room at the end. There was little sign of activity in this part of the house and they seemed to be the only ones around. They were intrigued and felt quite privileged to be granted the opportunity to try this fascinating concoction of their new found friends, for whilst they'd quite liked meeting some of the people in the party, neither of them were natural 'party-types' and the chance of a little respite from the crowded rooms downstairs came as something of a relief.

They were led into a small room with two armchairs and a small table in the centre. Having accepted the invitation to take their places in the chairs, they watched the couple reach down and withdraw a large greenish coloured bottle from a recess in the corner. They explained that the drink was a special fruit-based concoction with a slightly 'herby' quality to it. Two glasses appeared and Patrick and Norma watched as the husband poured a generous quantity of the dark mauve coloured drink into a glass and handed it to Patrick. He then repeated the process and handed the second drink to Norma who smiled politely and raised the glass to her lips for an initial sip. It was certainly an interesting flavour – a blackcurranty tang but with a bitter aromatic edge to it. Patrick raised his glass and followed his wife's example, sipping cautiously and patting his lips together to try to establish the exact flavour. It was certainly pleasant and at the encouragement of the couple not to 'stand on ceremony' they drank more earnestly.

It was about five minutes or so after the initial tasting, when each was about halfway down the glass that a slight wheeziness began to come across the pair of them; a light-headedness that made them feel a bit giddy and drowsy. They were a little startled, but felt that perhaps the excitement of the night and the demands of mixing with so many new people might just have taken it out of them and been a little too much for them.

They felt obliged to offer some apology, but were told not to even think about apologising. It had been a long day and they probably just needed to rest a while and then they'd be fine. In fact, there was a bedroom next door that they might as well pop into for ten minutes and take a lie down. Whilst neither Patrick nor Norma felt comfortable about having to take a reprieve in someone else's house; and in a bedroom at that, they certainly felt they would benefit from a period of repose and were beginning to experience a hazy, kind of floating sensation. It made them wonder if anything could have been in the drink they'd been given; but that was being suspicious and they really shouldn't allow themselves to think such thoughts.

It was from that point on, that Patrick had only vague recollections of being led singly from the room to an adjacent room, where, almost as soon as he'd been seated on the side of the bed, he began to feel as if under some kind of anaesthetic, not unlike the last few moments before finally going 'under' prior to an operation in hospital. He dragged his feet up onto the duvet and lay still, only partly aware of his surroundings and of the figure at his side, able to do little beyond lying in a semi-hallucinatory trance.

He had been only vaguely aware of the woman standing by him at first, looking down and then, moments later, crouching above him and reaching to start undoing the buttons on his shirt. He was dimly aware of it being removed and then – one by one – the remainder of his clothes. He had vague recollections of the woman removing her own clothes, joining him on the bed and beginning to trace down his body, first hands, then tongue; exploring whilst simultaneously fondling and caressing with urgent expertise.

She was, for sure, a seasoned practitioner in such matters – and almost immediately had him in the thrall of a series of involuntary spasms – exhaling in tight rhythmic gasps – reaching for her – drawing her to him – arching his back to meet her with wild convolutions of his hips and pleas for more. With a cry of exhilaration he lifted his hands to her shoulders as she rode him, bronco-style, urging him to fuck her. He duly obliged, until, midst a frenzy of whoops and yelps, like the cry of a wounded beast, he finally ejaculated deep and copiously into her inner being.

When he came round some thirty minutes later, he found himself alone on the bed. And with his mind, more or less free of the vagaries of the last forty five minutes or so and pretty much returned to full consciousness, he lay still and stared blankly at the ceiling – his brain locked in a desperate maelstrom of emotions, which – at that moment were too befuddled to even come close to taking any semblance of shape or order.

He emerged from the bedroom in a dishevelled state. He had no way of knowing what had happened to his wife and, at that moment, wanted little more than to make his exit with minimum delay. He checked his few belongings, which at least seemed to be intact, and descended the stairs and having made a brief and unsuccessful search for his wife, went straight out of the front door.

He arrived back at their house to find her slumped on the sofa. As he entered the room she looked up and then as quickly looked away, her hands covering her face. Neither of them spoke and for a minute he could do little but stand and watch, as she rocked herself back and forth in the depths of despair.

Even as he took his place on the end of the seat and raised an arm to her shoulder, he sensed the worst; she simply recoiled, curled into the sofa, weeping uncontrollably, her head buried in her hands.

It was an unbearable moment, riddled with guilt and yet compelled – he knew – to bear witness to the pain he had wreaked upon her – forced to share in the extent of her distress and misery; the very notion of commiseration or conciliation little more than abhorrent obscenities.

It was at first light the following morning that – at her behest – he followed her along the lane that would lead them to the path that eventually took them to the place – 'their' place. It was a steep climb but, on a morning such as this, neither of them seemed to notice. And for his part, he was only too happy to go along with anything that might see him on the path to forgiveness and ultimate redemption.

They made their way up the increasingly steeper slopes until, about ten or fifteen minutes later, they turned off the last bit of tarmac to climb the rocky crag that led them to the spot.

It was a favourite spot of theirs – a kind of balcony – or more a platform – a flat area of rock some forty feet wide and maybe ten feet from the side of the mountain to the edge of a six or seven hundred foot drop to the valley below. They had become regular visitors, feeling as they did, that its seclusion and position – high up in the lower mountains (the upper mountains being accessible only to expert mountaineers) offered a sense of peace and – being closer to God – an ideal forum for inner reflection and temporary sanctuary from the hurly-burly of daily life.

On this occasion they were, understandably, more subdued than elated and, for a moment, simply stood gazing in silence at the dark mountain slopes, already shrouded in a thin grey mist, making the jagged peaks invisible from where they were standing.

He had placed himself behind her in anticipation of what might be to follow, when she took a few steps to her right and stopped.

She turned, hesitating before she spoke.

'Darling...I'm sorry....' She was clearly struggling to find the words. Patrick, empathising with her struggle, took a step towards her, his arms raised.

'Darling....please......I___.'

'No.' She stopped him in his tracks, urging him to hold his ground. 'Darling....don't come any closer...please.' The pain was etched in every inch of her expression.

'There's a reason for bringing you here – something I haven't told you – about last night.'

He stopped – reaching now – urging himself to find the appropriate words.....

'It's alright darling...I understand.....God understands,' he cried, both arms extended – a plea for her to join him.

'No, you don't understand.'

She stepped more violently away from him, her voice now teetering on the brink. She took another step and turned to her right, breathing deeply.

'I'm sorry darling. I'm going to hate having to tell you this, but – as God is my witness – I must......It's the only way.'

With hands held tightly at her sides and tears streaming down both cheeks, she proceeded to recount how the previous evening – she couldn't be sure whether under the influence of something in the drink – but suffice to say, a man – *the* man – had taken her, under the fit of some strange hallucination, to the bed, where....she could barely bring herself to mouth the words....he had....undressed her.....and.....made unsolicited and improper advances....that...she hesitated, barely able to contemplate the admission that was to follow....she had warmed to, succumbed to, with gay abandon and lustful expletives....until finally being penetrated in the act of coitus, driven, it seemed, by most base and devilish thoughts.

At which point she looked up, forcing herself to bear witness to the pain she had wreaked upon him; to share the extent of his distress and misery – the very notion of commiseration or conciliation little more than abhorrent obscenities.

She turned quickly, shielding herself from the expression of horror fixed across every inch of his face.

'I'm sorry darling. I realised there could be no way back ....And now.....seeing it so clearly etched in every inch of your expression – I see it must be forever thus.'

This time, she didn't look up....

Without waiting for the tirade of remorse that would surely follow, she stepped to the edge and with her arms held out before her – leapt from the ledge into the surrounding air in search of redemption and she hoped – forgiveness in the eye of her Lord and Saviour.

Transfixed, as if in some smothering dream, her husband stepped to the edge of the precipice, his awe-struck, tear-stained eyes following the twirling, somersaulting body, as it plunged to the valley some six or seven hundred feet below, to its new-found haven of rocks and boulders.

He stood for a minute, head bowed, poised for a moment on the brink of the precipice – lost in a bottomless pit of despair.

Then, finally, he turned, head bowed, back to the path that would take him to the lane leading back down the mountainside.

＊ ＊ ＊ ＊ ＊

The Guy Upstairs and Albert

Like many anonymous souls who drift in and out of London's bedsit-land unseen and virtually unheard, Jed Noble lived a life of near-solitude, venturing from his room only occasionally, and then only to replenish his shelf with a few cans from the corner shop, or maybe, on a bright and breezy day, to sit amongst the pigeons on a park-bench opposite, where he might while away an hour or two watching the world pass by.

It was therefore something of an event, when – one typically grey November day – the peace and quiet of the house was shattered by the bizarre scene of Jed emerging from his room midst a maelstrom of faltering steps and the scraping of paws.

It was a ground-floor occupant John, who first witnessed the scene: the man who he knew only as – the guy upstairs – tugging on a piece of string with a small dog attached to its other end: as odd-looking a creature as you could imagine; its stumpy little body and sausage-length legs conspiring to make the whole business of movement a quite tangled and convoluted affair. One of its ears was strangely skew-whiff – almost back to front, as if, in its formative years, someone had grabbed it, twisted it and held on for dear life until it was firmly set in its reappointed direction.

John took a moment to take it all in. It was quite a performance, particularly as the pair set about negotiating the narrow staircase, and it was only after numerous yanks and pulls on the string and a number of expletives and admonishments, that they finally made it to the hallway to make their ramshackle exit through the door and onto the road.

He had named the dog Albert and it was to become a twice daily ritual, at around ten in the morning, and again at round five in the evening.

It was a few days later, that a small damp patch appeared in the top corner of John's bedsit room. Closer examination confirmed that the problem almost certainly stemmed from the flat above and that a little further investigation would be required.

It was with some trepidation that he mounted the stairs to make his way through the gloom to the end door of Albert and its owner.

He knocked and waited. It was some moments before the shuffling of feet was followed by the opening of the door and the half-appearance of a bedraggled face peering at him through the jamb. He explained briefly about the damp patch that had appeared on his ceiling before Jed, taking a moment for the point to register, shuffled back into the room, leaving the door open for John to follow.

In common with most bedsits, the room was economically furnished – a bed stuffed next to a wardrobe next to a single table opposite a sink, electric cooking rings and a grey and fraying carpet. Whilst above, a bare light bulb hung precariously from a single flex. A small window offered a hint of daylight, but it failed to reach all but a tiny corner of the room where a small rug hid a few glistening patches of what remained of the frayed and threadbare surface.

In the corner, a similarly functional kitchenette: sink, two cooking rings, tiny fridge and a square yard of working surface under two shelves which had been hurriedly and expediently screwed to the wall in reasonable proximity to the cooking rings.

Jed stood a moment and then peered in the direction John indicated and then shuffled his way towards the kitchen area and stopped by the sink, shifting a collection of cups and cutlery to one side.

The problem was immediately apparent – a tiny trickle of water droplets sliding down to nestle into a watery pool underneath a bend in the pipe. The whole area was saturated and squelched around their fingers on further investigation.

Jed muffled an apology and attempted to turn a nut midway down the pipe, but it only confirmed that the problem lay in a washer lower down. It didn't appear to be a major issue however; a towel wrapped round the base of the pipe would temporarily suffice and they'd inform the landlord in due course.

It was as they straightened themselves to the centre of the room that the small dog appeared from a folded blanket in the corner. For a moment it stood, rigid and still, like a tea-pot. Jed stopped, rigid and still, looking down and pointing.

'Albert,' he said, nodding and then leaning across for the kettle. 'You ain't met Albert.'

John looked down at the dog which at first remained glued to the spot, and then ventured towards the stranger, his nose pointing inquisitively towards his trouser leg.

'Hi Albert,' said John, observing the slight waddle as it stepped its way towards him.

'Funny looking dog ain't he,' said Jed, flicking the switch on the kettle. 'Dunno what make it is, some sort of mongrel I reckon....ain't you,' he said, directing the last two words pointedly in the animal's direction. The dog sniffed the air at the recognition it was being awarded, as Jed replaced the sugar on the counter.

'Ain't hardly got no legs,' he said, looking round again. 'Legless – permanently pissed.' He giggled and spooned coffee into a cracked mug, turning to John.

'You want a coffee?' he asked, spoon in hand.

John declined the offer whilst watching as the dog abandoned his trouser leg to resort to twitching its nose amongst the bits and bobs on the carpet.

'Called it Albert because that was my dad's name,' said Jed giving the mug a stir and watching the dog ferret its way around the cooking area.

'Albert Noble. Albert Noble of Rotherhythe. He wan't much better looking either – ugly old sod – same as his wife.'

He chuckled and turned to follow the dog's movements around one of the table's legs. 'Used to like sniffing around like Albert too – his wife I'm talking about; had her nose sniffing every which way place that woman.'

He laughed again, but a little too energetically this time, and it quickly mushroomed to a deep-chested coughing, prompting the appearance of a small blue pump which he immediately thrust into his mouth.

For a while he remained standing at the cooker rings clinging to the wall, allowing time for the inhaler to run its course. After which, he replaced the pump in his pocket, chuckled and continued stirring the coffee, whilst turning to chuck a thin wedge of bread crust, watching as the dog leapt at to take with a clean snap of its jaws. Within seconds the bread was annihilated, prompting the arrival of a second piece which was similarly dispatched.

'Look at 'im eat. Jesus, it'd eat anything. Don't get your wallet out or 'e'll 'ave it.'

Jed resumed his seat and with the food-supply seeming to have come to a halt, the pair were reduced to eyeballing each other, like two boxers at the weigh-in before a big fight, until, with little prospect of further activity, or maybe just wearying of the game, the animal ventured its way across the carpet in search of any tit-bits that might be on offer elsewhere, leaving Jed to watch-on and slap his thigh approvingly.

'How long you 'ad 'im?' John had been following the dog's progress across the carpet and had guessed Albert was a relative newcomer on the scene.

'Albert?.....'bout a week.'

Albert had ventured to an area closer to the sink, no doubt intrigued by the aromas of damp that seemed to emanate from around its base.

'Found 'im down the tip. I was ditching some wheel hubs for Micky O' Rourke – Do you know 'im? Down the car shed, down passed the pie and eel place - 'bout twenty yards down on the right hand side – small place. I was ditching these old wheel hubs when this little head appears from behind some old kettles and tea-pots. Fuck knows how it got there – head poking up right next door to a pan handle. I was going to leave it there, or maybe tell Micky. Anyway it drags itself out from behind this old pot – grubby as shit it was, and limping; looked like it might've been dumped there, along with a load of pots and pans. It crawls out from behind the fridge door; maybe hurt its leg when it had been dumped or cut itself on a pot or bit of glass or something.'

Tiring of its fruitless search the dog waddled its way towards a blanket folded in the corner next to the plug sockets.

'Crippled dog, 'aint you....crippled dog. Can't 'ardly walk,' Jed watched as it settled into place, its head rested on its paws.

He placed the mug on the floor, still wheezing slightly from his exertions.

'So I've ditched the wheel hubs and I'm turning to go and it starts following me, limping along behind me. So I get back up the alleyway – you know – runs round the back of the shops and there it is – still coming after me – limping along, dragging its foot – kind of wiping its arse along the ground, cos it aint 'ardly got no legs and one of em's 'urt. Ain't 'ardly got no ears too – one of 'em's fucked up – crooked. So I'm thinkin' what I'm goin' to do. Then I thought I might as well take 'im and see what to do with 'im. So instead of waitin' around all day for 'im to catch up, I grabbed 'old of 'im and carried 'im, cos 'e don't weigh much. So I'm going one way carrying a load of old wheel hubs, and going the other way carrying a fucking dog. Anyway, it wan't 'urt bad, just a graze. Wiped it with a tissue. Then it just plonked itself down, didn't wanna move – lazy sod.'

The dog – oblivious to it all – was firmly settled on the blanket, its head perched on its paws, eyes shut tight.

Jed took another drink and placed the mug at his side.

'You seen its ear; fucking thing's on wrong way round.' He chuckled and made a quick grab for the blue pump in his trouser pocket.

John was looking at his watch. The evening was getting on and it seemed an appropriate point to make his excuses and leave. They might have sorted the leak problem but it seemed wiser to involve the landlord; that's what landlords were for, after all. John offered to do the chasing up and made his way to the door, leaving Jed curled up on the chair – and Albert curled up on the blanket.

With the damp patch gradually rescinded little was seen of Jed and Albert, though you could occasionally catch the kerfuffle as the pair made their twice daily forays up and down the stairs.

It was at around six-o-clock one evening that there was a knocking at John's door.

He put the plates down and turned back into the room. Knocking on someone's door was virtually unheard of in the house and could only mean something was wrong.

He reached the door and opened it to see Jed standing in the half-light of the hall behind him.

For a few seconds he just stood wearing a blank expression.

"Ave you seen 'im?' he said finally, looking over John's shoulder into the room.

For a moment John was left to half-guessing as to whom he was referring.

'Albert', said Jed, looking back over his shoulder. 'He's gone.'

His hand held the evidence: one of those interwoven types of string, the strands plaited for strength. One end was hanging from his wrist, the end frayed and loose.

'String broke,' he said, gazing at the frazzled strands. 'We was up the gravestones and he was pulling to 'ave a piss over some jam jar, so I give 'im a tug, to bring him back and it broke and he went off bobbling about all over the place, ain't never seen 'im move so quick.'

He stopped, peering inquisitively over John's shoulder.

'Stupid sod. Ave you seen 'im?'

'No, he hasn't been round here.' John looked round in confirmation there was no way he could be skulking around behind him.

Jed looked back into the hallway. And then looked to catch John's eye.

'Will you 'elp me look for 'im? I'm gonna go back up the church and then maybe down the tip.' He had one hand stuck firmly in his coat pocket. The other was still dangling the length of string in the space between them.

John looked behind at one or two tasks that maybe wouldn't hurt for waiting half an hour or so.

'Okay. I'll just get my coat.'

Jed it was who led the way, shuffling over stones and peering down amongst clumps of grass and lines of withered flowers. John opted for the other direction, searching along the wall and then back over the rectangular frames to the church entrance.

Five minutes later they met up. Albert was nowhere in sight.

They changed directions – fanning out either side of the clock-tower, Jed leaning in and out of the bushes and looking ahead to where the fence met the main road. There was little to see except black stretches of undergrowth and the dark rectangles in the foreground. Jed finally shuffled his way out along the small path that led onto the main road.

'Fuck it, he ain't 'ere,' he said, reaching to his pocket for the blue pump. 'Stupid fucking dog.'

Almost immediately, they were back on the road, looking up and down and checking the guttering that bordered it.

The jagged angles of the tip heaped starkly, looking almost beautiful under the moonlight, as Jed furrowed his way over one to make his way towards the next. John took the other side – eyeing along the fence and checking for any movement around the area closer to the gate.

Jed eventually reappeared over a hill of wheels and discarded fridges, eyeing left, right and then back, grasping the pump and making his way to the gate.

With a final curse they moved towards the exit.

'Fuck it, let's get back. Maybe 'e's waitin' at 'ome.'

They took the alleyway back to the house.

Once there, Jed made a quick exit to the back, searching amongst the bushes and then another glance along the road. Albert was nowhere to be seen. They made their way to the front door, and with a mumbled thanks Jed climbed the stairs and disappeared into the gloom at the end of the landing.

It was a week or so later, that there was another knock at the door. John placed his duster to one side and went to answer it.

It took a while to recognise the face – it was the landlord. He lived some distance away and it was unusual to see him frequenting one of his lower-end-of-the-market properties such as this.

For a moment he shuffled awkwardly with a few papers and then drew a handkerchief and pen from his top pocket. He was a squat, busy man, with a predilection for getting his business done with minimum fuss or delay.

'That business with the damp....sorted?' he asked, glancing over John's shoulder and nodding in the general direction of the upstairs flat. John cast his eye over his shoulder and nodded.

'Yeh...It's cleared.'

'Good.'

The landlord stared down at a wad of paper and fumbled with his hanky.

'It was a washer on the pipe...easy sorted...no problem.' He looked again into the room and shifted from foot to foot.

'Everything all right?' He reached into his pocket, searching for another tissue which he partly opened in the palm of his hand.

'Yeh...all right. Nothing much happening really.' John watched as the landlord spread the tissue evenly beneath his nose.

Looking first along the hall, he looked back at the landlord and nodded towards the stairs.

'Is the guy upstairs still around?' he asked, casting his mind back to the episode with Jed and his dog, and in light of the fact that neither had been seen for a while.

The landlord brought the handkerchief up to his nose for a resounding blow before lowering it to examine the contents.

'Noble?...' He shrugged and crumpled his hanky into his fist. 'I see 'im when the pipe was fixed. Ain't seen 'im since.'

He shuffled a little more with the tissue and then looked at John, twirling the pen in circles next to his forehead. 'Bit sandwich short of a picnic...know what I mean....Bit nuts...You get 'em in these places.'

He replaced the pen in his top pocket and flipped the paper to the back of the pad. 'Has a problem with his lungs....been in 'ospital few times...carries this blue thing he shoves in his gob all day long.'

He reached into his trouser pocket to withdraw a fresh tissue which he held in readiness. And then popped the pad into his pocket.

'Do you know if he found his dog?' asked John, interested to get the low-down on Albert's last-known whereabouts.

The landlord placed the hanky under his nose to blow ferociously, before glancing down to do another check on its contents.

'Fat little bastard with the stumpy legs?.....He 'ad it upstairs in the room.'

'I know, it went missing – ran off.'

The landlord thought for a moment and brushed a few flecks off the lapel of his jacket.

'I told 'im no dogs. I told 'im when I sorted the washer out. No dogs allowed in the 'ouse; strict rule. It ain't 'ealthy. They got fleas, lice, shit, all sorts.'

He straightened his coat and looked down, tapping the door jamb with his foot.

'I see it next day.....when I was driving past to check the guttering up one of the 'ouses past the church....sniffing round the front door 'ere, like it's looking for somethin', mouse or something', piece o' string 'anging off its collar. So I parked up and nabbed it.'

He crumpled the soiled tissue and fisted it into a tight ball. 'Seen...grabbed it...' The tissue was quickly deposited into his pocket. '....Sorted.'

John stole a glance towards the stairs. The landlord looked over his shoulder into the room and nodded briefly.

'So..everythin's okay .....'

'Yeh,' said John.

The landlord turned to make his exit.

'Right, I'm on my way. Just thought I'd pop by, make sure the damp's sorted......Catch ya later...'

He bustled his way along the hall and, seconds later, was out of the door, closing it behind him.

John looked again in the direction of the stairs. He made his way along the hall, where he stopped a moment, looking up and listening for any sign of disturbance. He made his way up the stairs.

He could hear nothing and was about to make his way back when he turned, went to the door and knocked sharply. There was no response – no shuffling of feet, no sound whatsoever from within. He waited a moment longer and knocked again, a little more loudly. There was only silence. He remained a moment longer and then made his way back to his room.

During the days that followed the only disturbance in the house was the occasional opening or closing of a door and the tumble of letters through the mail-box.

John occasionally ventured round the corner to the mini-market replenish his shelf with a few cans and on a bright and breezy day, maybe sit amongst the pigeons in the park opposite to while away an hour or so watching the world pass by.

It was one morning, about a week later that there was a kerfuffle on the stairs – the sound of shuffling and then a clattering and banging and a number of oaths in raised voices. John poked his head from his room.

It was a couple, a youngish couple – early twenties. They stopped at the bottom of the stairs before beginning the business of heaving the first of two large cases to the upstairs landing. From his doorway John watched as they eventually managed to get both suitcases to the top of the stairs and drag them along the landing to the door at the end, where they stopped a moment to catch their breath, before opening the door with their new key. John turned back into his room and locked his door behind him.

The Stationmaster

Joe Atkinson, the stationmaster, stooped his way through the green wooden doors of the station entrance, dragging the broom behind him. He stopped a moment to ease the brush end through the gap. There were no passengers at this time of night; it was some twenty minutes or so since the last train had eased its way from Platform Two towards the cutting in the gloom of the woods, on its way to the stretches of fens and marshes to its ultimate destination.

The station itself was in fact little more than a rectangular entrance area of huge slabs of stone built some hundred and fifty or so years ago. Photographs of the various stages of the station's history were a permanent fixture on display above the fireplace and the whole interior was, in its way, its own miniature museum-piece – an iconic 'throwback to the past' midst the ever-changing world beyond its walls. A single bulb hanging from a flex in the centre of the wooden slatted ceiling, cast the whole area in a golden glow, which – in December – was like a village theatrical setting for the nativity itself.

Against a wall, under a tiny fluorescent strip in the model stable roof, a tiny basket and surrounding pot-figures of wise-men adopted their annual position in a shoe-box of straw surrounded by fairy lights. A small brown painted collection box stood at its side, all contributions heading for a hospice at nearby Allensdale. Set in the wall to the right, the small ticket window was bordered by slightly drooping silver and green tinsel bathed in a rectangle of light from behind.

On the opposite side, a small iron pot of red-hot coals glowed and brought an old-fashioned warmth into the sharp chill of the late December evening.

The pot, or more precisely, the base upon which it stood, was partly Joe's own work. A rather rickety contraption when delivered two and a half years ago from a metal merchants at High Mowbray; he'd soldered and bolted an arrangement of metal legs and supporting stanchions to its base to form a firm stand for it to sit on over at the side by the fireplace. It had been a relatively straightforward task using some of the collection of tools that he had accumulated over the years and still kept in the utility shed for use as and when required. Being something of a 'handyman', he'd taken some pride in his solid sturdy handiwork that had already seen its way through a couple of winters.

He took the broom in both hands and began sweeping the floor in steady systematic movements, beginning at the area under the timetable board and working his way slowly over to the tiny Christmas tree – an annual gift from the Legion of the neighbouring village – and then back to the wall and across to the now redundant fireplace in the wall opposite. As he swept, he hummed a vague resemblance to 'Silent Night', partly to alleviate the dull ache that always gnawed its way across the small of his back round about this time of evening, a trademark of many, as they approached their doting years.

He completed his sweeping and turned rather awkwardly through the door to the platform itself where the open air was already laced with an encroaching mist. He cast his eyes to where a light flurry of snow danced and twirled from the mist through the platform lights like an invading army of tiny moths. Whether it would make any lasting impression remained to be seen. Shivering and with shoulders hunched against cold and back-ache, he worked his way along the platform's length, sweeping a few ticket stubs and wrappers and the thin white dust with methodical right to left sweeps of the brush, stopping momentarily to reach for the hanky and dab the end of his nostrils.

He glanced at his watch. Eight forty three...and counting! There already seemed to be an easing in the snow.

As he reached the platform's end he looked back and could see that virtually nothing had replaced it. Nonetheless, as he made his way back to the door, he swept the brush both left and right just to make sure the surface was free.

Back in the station foyer he replaced the broom and turned his attention to the coffee pot still steaming on the table by the entrance. A regular and popular feature of the station – the coffee pot stood on its tiny wooden table, bubbling its way through the day, available for anyone who cared to partake. A little jug of milk at its side and bowl of sugar completed the picture. You popped fifty p in the box, as your contribution to a local charity and took your place on the platform. Every evening at eight-forty five Joe turned the dial to zero and switched the machine off in preparation for lifting the heavy dome from its base into the back room. A few cups would be rinsed under the single tap and the jug emptied, rinsed and placed on the shelf for tomorrow.

He hummed another tune vaguely reminiscent of 'Jingle Bells' as he wiped the table and popped the tea and table cloths in their place on the shelf. The computer screen still shone into the office area.

It had taken him a while to bring himself up to date with the weird and wonderful ways of the modern transport system, but with a bit of help from the lads at the Edenbridge station, next up the line, he'd been able to, if not 'master', at least 'come to terms with' the basic functions.

As he moved the tray of pens to one side, he chuckled at recollections of writing tickets by pen and popping half-crowns and three-penny pieces between the wooden slats in the drawer. He winced slightly as he straightened his back and made his way once more toward the door to the platform. It wasn't that his back was necessarily getting worse, but it sometimes seemed that way, particularly with these freezing temperatures that they'd been stuck with these last few days;

'global warming' - that was what it was all about; and those 'greenhouse gases'. It seemed strange to be talking of 'global warming' on such days as this.

He made his way toward the end of the nearside platform to the gate by the ivy tree. He checked the lock and swept a few thin wafers of snow off the bars of the gate. Having locked the door to the utility shed and still stepping lightly, he made his way back to the main entrance.

There was little prospect of much more happening tonight. The only interruption would be the 'Inter-City' from London, passing through on Platform Two.

He pulled his thick *Railnet* coat a little higher over his shoulders and lifted the notice-board through the door into the foyer area. Christmas was not far down the line and he grimaced at the prospect of the fuss that usually accompanied it. His brother would be over and there'd been rumours of Michael and Eve making it from Australia, though he'd be surprised if they did; if anything, the kids were still a bit young. He'd half a mind to go out to Australia himself some day to see them – just a 'one-off' – be the only time he'd get there. But he wasn't sure about having to sit on a plane all that time. Boxing day he'd be going over to Eleanor's at Fensome. Barry'd come and get him and the wife and with a bit of luck they'd pop in 'The Bull' for a quick one before facing the commotion at home.

He lifted the rack of leaflets on *Things To Do And See* and placed it behind the trellis door along with the ladders and spare boards for updates on current situations like snow interruptions or ice on points or 'leaves on the line' - he always chuckled at the way the papers got hold of that one.

He glanced at his watch again and checked it against the twenty-four hour clock fixed high on the wall above the computer screen. The *IC* would be passing through shortly.

He often stood in the doorway and watched it thunder its way between the two platforms – his own little mark of respect, though he didn't, in real terms, feel any particular sense of deference. To him it was just a long line of fancy boxes, with some fancy table lights chucked in for good measure.

He turned back to the office and set about wiping the first of the three work-surfaces with a cloth – carefully arranging the carbon-backed ticket pad against the wall under the ring file.

The unused tickets were neatly stacked and placed in two piles in the left hand drawer next to the 'pin & pencil' drawer where he popped the pens and pencils that had found a use during the course of the day. The third section of the drawer was for pins, adhesives and various 'bits and bobs' that came in useful for the notice board and 'Coming Events' corner by the entrance. He took the key to the wall cupboard from the nail at its side and locked away the timetables and work-schedules for the coming quarter. A quick glance at his watch confirmed he could do the totals for the day's tickets – a fairly quick, routine procedure now that he'd become familiar with it.

That done, he made his way out onto the platform and took the bucket from the side by the traffic cone shed. It was a bit of a struggle, the bucket full of sand and grit weighed heavily and he had to watch his footing up the slight incline to the main surface of the platform.

He stopped several times and stood up straight to ease the discomfort in his back. But it had to be done. In the morning there would be passengers waiting for their train and it was his responsibility to ensure they could wait in safety. There was always the possibility of further snow, perhaps a heavy fall, which could harden over night and water patches would be likely to freeze over completely. It was his responsibility to make sure the customers were protected. He contemplated a kettle of boiling water but that would just cool and possibly add to the iciness. He would have to treat it with the gravel mix he'd prepared back in October in readiness for the winter months. He had mixed the gravel by hand to ensure he got the correct blend of small, medium and larger (but not too large) stones, then mixed it with appropriately graded sand, a particularly coarse sand from a builder's yard in Northslade. The result was a rough and coarse mix that was 'almost' slip-proof.

He placed the bucket on the platform to catch his breath and wipe a small bead of water from the chilled end of his left nostril. There was a correct way of dispensing the gravel. No way would he use a trowel; you didn't get sufficient control over it and you couldn't guarantee that each and every part of the platform would receive the required amount of gravel to make it safe.

Instead he took a handful of the mix – no gloves of course, they also hindered the process and with the bucket over one arm he took slow easy steps to maintain his footing and made regular sweeping movements with his other hand, spraying the stony mixture evenly over every square foot of the platform. After several steps he stopped and took the hanky from his pocket to dab once again at the point of his nose.

He glanced at his watch. He hesitated by the entrance to the *Gents* - it certainly wouldn't be used again this evening – but there was always tomorrow, people could slip on the surface in the freezing morning if he didn't treat it. He ventured round the corner and threw handfuls of grit over the area in front of the urinals. It took a minute or so to complete his slow amble to the end of the platform, still spreading the grit around him in regular spiral movements.

It was as he turned to make his way back down the platform, still spreading the areas that seemed a little bare, that he heard the rumble of the *IC* and stopped to watch as, seconds later, the surrounding trees were fleetingly illuminated by the carriages' lights.

He had made several further steps towards the doors to the foyer and was about to look up to watch the train speed its way through when he suddenly went deaf.

He would remain deaf for another ten to fifteen seconds as an explosion of cataclysmic proportions shattered the station and the surrounding area for several hundred yards.

His final movement was little more than an involuntary flinch, after which, he knew nothing.

It was about a week later that the head-bowed and slightly nervous representative of *Railnet* followed Joe's widow through the dimly-lit hallway to the lounge, where, at her invitation he took a seat on one of the two armchairs that faced the settee. There was little light in the room. The curtains had remained drawn for some days.

Mrs. Atkinson hovered above the settee, her right hand resting on the top corner. She offered him a cup of tea. He declined the offer. She eased herself down into the settee, almost, it seemed, deliberately squeezing herself up against its left arm.

She was small and frail-looking, particularly in the thin curtained light of the room. A small bonnet of white hair topped her rounded, slightly podgy face, the eyes indistinct and staring out into the room, and then at her visitor, her fingers clasped tightly.

The *Railnet* representative coughed and adopting what he hoped was an appropriate pose, proceeded to offer the condolences of the company. She nodded, offered a barely audible 'thankyou' and waited for him to continue.

Attempting to address her directly, he clarified the basic cause of the accident: in simple terms – a loosened rail due to a broken bolt some twenty yards or so from the end of the platform. He explained that the fault had been communicated to Head Office but since their company didn't actually 'fix' the faults, it was a different company's responsibility to oversee it.

He paused for a second, directing his attention to the brass handles on the sideboard, and upon it, a photograph of the village station – taken in 1920 – and underneath a fine-line pen drawing of one of the old steam-engines – possibly the 'Flying Scotsman' itself.

Returning to the matter in hand, he explained that the fixing of things like bolts on the rails was the responsibility of a company called *South Eastern* Lines, but the problem had been that whilst it was down to *South Eastern Lines* to fix the bolt, they sub-contracted some parts of the network to a firm called *Railfix* based at Tonbridge.

Mrs. Atkinson sat twining and untwining her fingers in increasing tempo as he spoke. The representative coughed nervously and looked towards the brass handles on the sideboard.

He explained that whilst *Railfix* provided things like the bolts on the sleepers, a firm of 'toolmakers and engine designers' in Redhill provided the tools and they'd met with a number of contractual complications due to a shortage of toolmakers...And consequently there'd been difficulties in meeting the orders and ....as a consequence, the bolt on the line hadn't got round to being fixed.

He looked at Mrs Atkinson, who sat for a moment, contemplating his explanation, but saying nothing.

When she eventually looked up, it was with some considerable effort and in a visibly faltering voice that she thanked him for taking the trouble to come and inform her. He, in turn, thanked her and once again offered his and the company's sincere condolences.

As he stood and straightened his coat, he explained that the company would be in contact, regarding compensation and the details of her husband's pension and insurance arrangements. He looked quickly away, before making his way down the hall to the door.

Before he reached for the knob of the lock he stopped and turned to face her.

'I'm sorry Mrs. Atkinson.'

It was as he turned to go that she laid a hand on his arm and made a start forwards.

'Tell me....' she said. 'I've listened to everything you've said and I've understood what you've been telling me but there's something I don't quite understand.'

He turned to observe the glazed, questioning look in her eyes.

'Joe had plenty of bolts for the sleepers and all sorts of other things and lots of tools. He kept them in his shed at the station. He'd have gladly put one in for you if you'd have asked him. He was good at things like that; he always has been. It wouldn't have been any trouble.'

For a moment their eyes met.

'Well....' He tried, but the words had finally given up on him. He stared at a picture pinned on the wall about halfway down the hallway. It showed a windmill on top of a cliff, with a thick blue sky and bright sun in the background.

'It's just that nowadays things aren't as simple as that I'm afraid Mrs. Atkinson,' he said ... 'I'm sorry.'

At which, he turned to make his way through the door and down the path, leaving her standing in the door frame.

* * * * *

The following year a new chrome-panelled station opened to replace the one that had been destroyed in the disaster. It incorporated the latest 'hi-tec' 'state of the art' computer technology for ticket-sales and access to timetable and general information regarding rail travel on current *Railnet* schedules. It was opened by Sir Michael Prendergast – Managing Director of *Railnet*. A small plaque had been bolted into the lower section of panelling opposite the ticket office thanking Joe for his contribution to the company.

The Wishing Well

A man, clad in a mourning-grey smock, sat cross legged on an easy stool. He slid a glass of elderberry water to one side and flicked to the next page of the pamphlet that had seen him through the last half hour or so, and would likely see him through the next.

To his immediate left was a squared grill – an arrangement of criss-cross metal gauze set in the deep space between two flanks of a protruding wall. The grill itself had been expediently placed at eye level above the stool upon which he was seated. A single black curtain draped from an overhead rail, stood drawn and idle, removing the left flank of the grill from sight. The man yawned and turned to the next page. His world surrounded him, a non too-inspiring world, comprising, as it did, little more than a twenty foot cell arranged around the stool upon which he was seated and the grill at his side. Beyond this, a 'sleeping quarter', a sister cell, less than ten feet square and steeped in perpetual darkness, save for a slither of light that crept through a tiny window at ceiling height.

From his vantage point by the grill, he could keep a semi-redundant eye on the oaken door opposite and the tiny side window at its side, through which – in moments of repose – he could observe the passing clouds and vague shimmers of a distant sun.

The man turned the page and reached for the remains of the drink.

As he did so, a rustling noise drew his attention to the door, which faltered slightly before the falling of a catch prompted its opening. He raised an eye, placing both pamphlet and glass to one side.

A swell of sunlight filled the cell. And amidst it, silhouetted in the crescent light of the porch – a bowed figure of a man.

The man hesitated a moment – wary, at first, of venturing too far into the sepulchral gloom, but able still to make out the figure seated somewhere behind the wire-meshed grill at the far end of the cell. Reassured that he had likely found the right place, he stepped further into the beam of light as if to confirm his presence.

His nervous eyes roved the scene, settling eventually on the small stool that was a permanent fixture on the nearside of the grill.

He shuffled across the stone floor towards it and having reached its proximity, a pantomime-like silence ensued, as each waited for the other to break the spell, prompting the figure behind the curtain to level an invisible arm in the vague direction of the stool.

'Take a seat my friend and the weight off your evidently over-burdened feet.'

It was strange hearing the words from a bearer so effectively shielded from sight: clear and demonstrative enough in tone, yet secreted behind the hanging curtain and inconspicuous to all before it – an anonymity which seemed to lend a stronger resonance and had the man scuttling to the stool, which – with the sun in its dying throes – was at once cast in a pool of yellow light. Once seated, he coughed nervously and hung his head toward his lap.

It was clearly a pained and distressed figure that the man had seated before him. But what was equally clear, was that the man was no local figure. He could tell it at a glance, for time had taught him to identify every straggly beard and blank washed-out expression in the village and for some way beyond it; indeed, their lily-livered whingeings were, by now so familiar to his ear that he had often been of a mind to gather his belongings to try his luck amongst the sheep-shearers and cattle-men of the next county.

No, this man was clearly a stranger – the stooping shoulders and slow shuffling gait told of a journey of quite likely some several miles.

He allowed the man a moment's grace before leaning forwards to draw the crouched figure closer to the curtain.

'Gather yourself my son, and speak of the plight that has brought you such distance as to warrant a place on the stool upon which you are perched.'

The man sniffled and raised an eye.

'Well Father,' he began. 'It is a matter of much lament that brings me here. A matter that to you, may be little in tales of woe, yet to me tells of a future drowning in sorrow and grief.'

The Father took a moment to drain his glass and hold an eye on this forlorn figure now taken to rocking back and forth on the stool like a child in a state of distress.

'Well come man – collect your spirits and speak. For as bleak as you may picture your plight, successors to your stool will likely bear tales more hopeless than the one you are poised to tell. Speak up.'

There was a grimace of doubt as to this, but nonetheless the man, raised himself a tad to set about unloading his soul of its lamentable baggage.

'It's.....my wife,' he said, struggling to look the Father in the eye, his voice weak and wavering, like that of an ailing chicken. 'I live by the village of Assenti, some ten miles distance across the plains and peat-woodlands. I have – or just about have – a small-holding – chickens, a few pigs, a cluster of sheep and small graze of cows. It isn't much, but it suffices.' He hesitated, struggling to assemble his plight into some sense of order. 'And....I have had money....not a lot, but enough; enough that is...before I succumbed Father...succumbed to temptation.'

At which point the man crumpled to a tiny ball, his wiry fingers clasping at tufts of hair in a fit of exasperation and grief. It was some moments before he felt able to continue....

'But all this Father, matters little to me when it comes to my wife – my dear wife – as lovely a woman as ever set foot beyond the banks of the Jusenti river.'

He paused – time enough for the unyielding image of a beautiful woman to cross both their paths.

'It was a time of richness and gaiety that I met her. And with much happiness and joy that she drew herself to my side to make our mark on our future.....And yet, here we are some miniscule way into our bond.....and...it is gone – that warmth of spirit evaporated into the air. And – it seems – my beautiful wife set to follow it.'

He looked up beseechingly, searching for any glint of light amongst the dark forbidding bars.

'The thing is Father.....I've always done my best to please her, to tend to my duties as a husband should – to make her a happy contented woman....I cut the grass by our homestead to keep it neat and tidy; milk the cow at six-thirty each evening and bring the filled urn dutifully to the table....I've plugged every gap at ceiling level with wads of pillowing to keep roof-insulation at a level any woman would expect her man to maintain ....And yet....all this...it seems, is not enough. For all my endeavours, my wife – seems – with her endless bouts of unbroken silence – to taunt me of a sad and fallow existence, and to bring such pressure on my soul, that I have been quite at my wit's end.'

It was all too much for the man who took his moment to sink his head in a fit of uncontrollable weeping.

'Fear not,' said the Father, leaning to where the heavy sobs continued to drift under the satin drape. 'In speaking your mind you are already some way to freeing it from the turmoil of grief. It is the way of the world in these things and there's no shame to be taken.'

The words at least seemed to stir the man to some defence of his case.

'Well it's good of you to say it Father, and may I add that, in matters of the heart, I have done my bit: upon her each and every birthday – a pink carnation sits upon her place-mat – and

never a day nor hour nor minute too late.....And yet, even then, she says nothing, but merely weeps at the window, gazing out across the paddock toward the distant plain and woodland.'
The man turned an eye toward the cell window. And then he turned and raised his face once more to the grill.
'So Father.....and I come to what is perhaps the crux of my point. I can only perceive that it must all come down to that root of most ills...Money....for I am not a rich man, and will concede that, with the failing of crops from such drought as we have had, I have had my share of toil in keeping the wolf at bay. But...It is an issue Father, to which I have awarded much thought, being as I am, far from feckless in these matters.....'
At which point he shuffled forwards, his fall from grace not yet entirely complete...
'Until, one day it struck me that I might take myself to the village, where word has it, the 'money-men' of our land sit, biding their time, waiting their opportunity – how do they put it? – to make mountains from our molehills. And, accordingly, I entrusted my small bounty to their care, that they might swell it to something as might at least bring some colour to the cheeks of my dear wife. But – alas – on my next visit, some two weeks hence, where my investments should have flourished, there was nothing, save a few crumbs and a few kopecks on a plate. It was a gamble Father....and it failed. And that – it seems – has been the way of my world.....And now....my wife....my beautiful wife...is set to leave me, to head off back to the village of Paxos, where she will, by all accounts, be 'at one' with her new life; a life that, sadly, will have no place for me.'
The Father, who had remained silent throughout the man's outpouring, reached for the elderberry wine bottle – a stiffer alternative to his daytime sustenance. He poured a glass and then a second which he passed under the grill to the trembling fingers behind the curtain. The man eyed the emerging hand, took the glass and drank eagerly.
And then, empowered no doubt by the drink, he looked up.

'Tell me Father.....for it is evident that I have sinned......and that sin lies at the core of all that ails me......but, what must I do?......I know that it was wrong to throw in my lot with the money-men, to have others make my fortune from nothing – to gamble my life away – but tell me what I must do to amend for my sins – to turn my wife's eye once more in my direction.'

The man was quite clearly at his wit's end, his eyes brimming at the prospect of an empty, wife-less life – a soulless existence, devoid of meaning or purpose....

'My beautiful wife, raven-haired and alabaster-skinned – please...I'll do anything Father.....anything.'

The Father reached once more for his glass, smacked his lips and then lowered an eye to the fringe of the curtain, ushering the man closer, to a point where their expressions were no further apart than a width of satin.

'Sir'........he began, the words forming in his mind even as he was speaking.......

'Sin, being the building-block of our existence and as prevalent in our daily lives as the mere drawing of breath, may not yet have taken such root as you imagine; be brave – and not yet too dismayed, for all may not yet be lost.....'

He stopped in readiness to deliver the words that would, with luck, pave the way to the man's redemption and ultimate salvation.

'Sir.....You must make your way to the mountain of Zamia....to the Well that you will find there at its peak – a simple stone affair that, for all its humble appearance, is in truth, a temple – The Temple Of Eden – You may be familiar with its modern-day impostor currently masquerading under the title in our capital city.'

He took a quick drink from the glass and leant his head a little nearer to the curtain....

'And once there, you must drop a silver coin into the deep cavernous space, and with a single voice, directed to the bowels of the Well – plea for forgiveness with the clear words – '*Hail To Zania And To The Spirit Of Zania – I Come To Be Saved*'.

He drew an ear to the curtain tassels, urging the words' repetition from behind the screen.

'Hail To Zania And To The Spirit Of Zania – I Come To Be Saved...' returned the voice, taking some pride at having grasped it at the first attempt.

'That's right,' said the Father. 'Three times you must utter these words – and then you must return to your good lady wife with a wholesomeness and vigour as has been your style since the day dot. But....'

He leant forward once more and whispered closer into the bars of the grill...

'You must have patience, for these things are apt to take their course. But if – beyond the passing of a week or so – things show little sign of finding their feet – make your return and we'll take our discourse from there.'

The man was quick to concur and having slipped his coin beneath the curtain, that was the man's fee for his trouble, leant one last time to the grill, that his words be sure to find their target.

'Thank you Father.....Thank you...Thank you....For I am but a simple man....and though so clearly wrecked with sin, am at last – in the wake of your words of wisdom – set on the path to salvation with a freshness of mind and resurgence of spirit.'

'Good man...good man..'

A final farewell and he was gone, and the catch was dropped. The father emptied the last vestiges of elderberry wine and reached for his pamphlet.

It was only by the illuminating lantern of the moon that Nemo (the man's name was Nemo) finally made his way to the summit of the hill, where – true to the Father's words – he found a small circular stone affair set amongst a smothering of small bushes and reeds. This was clearly the place. There were no instructions or deliverances to be seen, but it was very much as the padre had described it.

He withdrew his purse and, as instructed, took a single silver coin, which he held briefly in the palm of his hand, wishing a rekindling of spirit into its still and lifeless form, before releasing it into the awning that was the space of the Well. If he expected a splash or even a 'plop' of some sorts, he was disappointed, for he was greeted with little beyond a deafening silence. He waited some moments and then leant over the blackness of the hole and released the words as firmly and distinctly as his breath could utter......
'Hail To Zania And To The Spirit Of Zania – I Come To Be Saved...' Three times – with appropriate intervals between – did he speak the line – his head hovering above the circle of brickwork in each case.

That done, he stared at the moon, fancying he could already see some fiercer glow in its silvery beacon, and then quickly withdrew and made his way down the hillside.

It was upon the sixth day, as the sun waned to its place across the stone floor, that the catch lifted and the figure re-entered his former domain.

It was, alas, with little lightness of foot or cheer, that he dragged himself across the space toward the stool.
The Father, eyeing the sun's rays suddenly flooding his cell, did a quick switch of water to wine and slid his pamphlet to one side, whilst ushering the man to his accustomed position on the stool. The man wasted no time in spilling his beans.
'Father.....forgive me, for I am Nemo....the sinner... you'll remember me from some days past when I shared with you the extent of my misery.'
The Father nodded and waited for his guest to compose himself sufficiently to continue. He poured two glasses of wine and eased one under the satin curtain.
'Thank you Father....Thank you.' The man reached for the glass and quickly lifted it to his dry and scaling lips. He sniffed and looked up, knowing it was clearly down to him to 'break the ice'.

'Well Father.....I made my way to the Well at Zania and followed your instruction to the letter, before making my way home to meet my wife with the courtesy and good humour you spoke of....'

He hung his head, the recollection, even then, almost catching in his throat...'And yet Father...it has made little difference.'

He stared blankly...his arms folded across his knees...

'In fact....no difference...truth be told. As ever, my wife says little and spends her time moping at the window, her mind fixed on some vague point on the horizon, but though I have looked in its direction, I cannot, for the life of me, make out what it might be...and I have given it the time you advised.'

He sighed, casting a haggard look in the Father's direction.

'But it seems the game's up Father. My wife is already lost, for she has taken her wares from the wardrobe and has already seen fit to utter word of her imminent departure to the village of Paxos.'

He sighed again and reached for the glass.

'My sins, it seems, are greater than I had taken them for.....I'm a lost man Father...and doubly so...with my money skittering around somewhere in the upper echelons of space...'

He placed the glass upon the shelf at his side ....

'Tell me Father....Where did I go wrong? There must be something... Something that I forgot or overlooked... Something that might yet rid me of the sin that already has my wife heading for a new beginning in Paxos?'

The Father clicked his tongue and turned his eye to the lower region of the wire-meshed grill.

'Well sir, first let us attempt to keep composure in line. For as I have said, these issues can often be set to linger a while before they're broken.'

He drew his eyes across the tips of his fingers, which he brushed back and forth in tiny whispery movements.

'It may be we need to turn our minds a little to this wife of yours – to see what lies at the root of her disenchantment.... Take your time now and let's hear a little more – of her manner and disposition – and those flowing locks which I recall you alluding to quite lyrically on our previous meeting.'

Glass in hand and feet up, the Father leant back to take on-board the next stage of his afternoon's work.

There was, at first, some uncertainty from Nemo who had rarely been called upon to give such a blow-by-blow account of his wife.

'Well….as I have made plain…..she is, for sure, a woman of true and radiant beauty – raven-black hair sunk to the narrow nape of her shoulders – as lithe as a gazelle – yet full-breasted and slender of hip. And her eyes Father – are sparkling sapphires that glint and gleam like the jewel in Cleopatra's belly.'

Twirling the glass in his fingers, The Father leant himself a little closer to the grill.

'And yet, by all accounts, a placid woman and quite untroubled by temperament,' he added, quick to complete the picture that was evidently at the heart of the man's despondency.

'Well sir…she has certainly been a somewhat lacklustre soul of late. But do not be fooled here; for she has a firmness of spirit – where I suppose I am lacking – being a sinner of such gaping magnitude.'

'Hmm…' The Father frowned, shuffling the glass to one side to move a little closer to the grill.

'Well then sir, another matter….'

He coughed and bowed his head as if in advanced apology for bringing such matters to light.

'How is it sir….in 'matters of the flesh', if you'll catch my drift?….It is an issue we men are often loathe to make public, yet, you'll concede it may hold some weight in your case.'

The man shifted himself closer to the curtain, almost seeming to welcome discussion of the matter.

'Of course Father, there's little to be gained in hedging around such issues…but there's little to tell…certainly no cause for concern in *that* respect…..For, on the night in question – being the first of each and every calendar month – my wife lies ready

and near-rigid in anticipation – and before there's even time to
point the snake at bell-jar, I'm done: in – out – as snug as a
blade in butter – no fuss – no bother. No sir...I think we can,
with some surety, say that 'the boxes are well and truly ticked'
in that department.'
The Father thought for a minute, brought the glass to the shelf
and, as if to swat the issue once and for all, lowered his eye to
the lower folds of the curtain.
'Well......my son...it's something of a mystery to be sure....Let
us take ourselves back to the night in question.....You found
the Well....You made your plea...you proffered the
coins......I___'
The man had suddenly leant himself to the grill.
'One moment Father....did I hear you say something of *coins*?'
The Father drew closer.....
'The confirmation – you'll remember I told you to commit a
number of coins – a mark of redemption en-route to the
absolution of sin.'
There was, at once, pandemonium behind the grill – as the
man's eyes widened toward the curtain.
'I have no recollection Father of the tumble of coins of which
you speak; 'coin' – for sure. Perhaps it passed me by in my
misplaced temper at the time.'
The Father clapped a hand firmly upon his cassocked knee.
'Sir.....Then there we have it.! You have missed the crux of
your confession sir....How can The Spirit know of your intent
without the confirmation of your commitment? Sir....you must
return to the Well, make your plea once more and be sure to
mark it with *several* coins, tossed with a graceful sweep of the
hand.....Only then can the path to forgiveness be laid bare!'
There was a short delay as the listener practised the movement
with shaking fingers behind the curtain grill.
'Sir, without delay you must make your return....But.....'
He stopped again and beckoned an invisible finger in the man's
direction. Nemo leant to a hair-breadth's distance behind the
satin. The Father's words were hushed.

'It might perhaps be expedient to bless the Well with something more than a mere palm-load of coins on this – the second occasion – if you get my drift....For why sacrifice the donkey for the sake of adjusting the weight on its back?'

At which point, Nemo, visions of his flaxen-haired beauty tumbling into his outstretched arms, fumbled at his bum-belt; money being no stumbling block in pursuit of his damsel's return.

'Tell me what you have my friend.....how many coins currently bless your purse?'

There was a split-second investigation....

'Well....I think eleven or so remain in place at the last count.'

'Ahh...No worries sir...that should do fine...or shall we say 'ten' pitched into the darkness would certainly help bring us a little closer to our self-appointed destiny......'

The man was ecstatic.

'Father.....how can I thank you?......You are the very font of kindness and courtesy...God bless you!'

'And you too my friend....but tarry not, for the sun's already upon the far wall of the cell...Be gone to Zania and then once more about that merry wife of yours.'

There was a whoop from beyond the curtain, as Nemo abandoned his stool and with the door clanking shut behind him, was out in the late evening air.

The Father took a moment for reflection, but decided against recalling the fellow for the kopeck that should by rights have found its way under the curtain.

It was at about four-o-clock in the afternoon some five days later, that – with hopefully sufficient time elapsed – the Father rose from his stool one last time and finished gathering his few belongings in an old knapsack. A few bottles of elderberry wine found their place beside his cassock belt and as a final act – the pamphlet was taken outside, to be discarded along with the others on a pile half-hidden at the foot of the garden.

Though a long wait, it had certainly had its moments. He looked across the barren décor that had been his home for as long as he cared to remember, and lifted the sack to its new-found place over his shoulder.

As the sun was set to breach its way to the oak and send its beam one last time across the cell floor, he left the grill, made his way to the door and stepped out into the early evening air, locking the door firmly behind him.

First stop would be at the hill to gather the 'collection' and from there he would make his way to the land beyond the Jusenti river – to the village of Paxos – where – with luck – a new life awaited.

✻ ✻ ✻ ✻

Trench Warfare

Corporal Dingle clambered across yet another heap of mud and forcing himself to lie as still as possible, gazed across the wilderness of busted holes and torn earth – and the ever-lingering odour of death. And cows...for some reason it was always the cows that hung around in the air the longest!

It had been some time since he had first lost his bearings amidst cross-fire barrages of machine-gun fire and artillery shells, and still had little choice than to lie still and wait.
For how long remained to be seen, but to attempt to move at that moment or to even raise his head a fraction, would be tantamount to suicide

He did a quick check on a few 'essentials': first-aid pack, whistle, hand grenade, binoculars and the rest, pressing himself as flat as possible into the slimy surface of wet dirt. As he lay there, easing his fingers down his side and into his pocket, he came across the compo biscuit – still hard and dry as a chunk of old chip-board. He eased its corner to his lips and tried to bite a piece off. But it was no easy task. He contemplated dipping it in the tiny pool of water by his chin in the absence of tea – sucking the brown, scaly compound until a gritty mix of biscuit and dirt had left his fingers, leaving thin traces of pink.

He was one of a patrol of six that had, some hours ago, been sent out to try to establish the situation regarding some enemy positions. Initially, it had involved negotiating a length of wire and then taking advantage of whatever appropriately sized craters could be accessed.

But even before they'd begun to find their feet in their new positions, the latest barrage had started and in customary fashion he'd been down in seconds, down in the nearest fox-hole; a different one to the others on this occasion, where he'd been obliged to do the only sensible thing – lie still for as long as it takes – and wait...and hope.

It is said that in such moments of extreme danger, past lives can swiftly pass through the mind. In his case, as he lay – the familiar surge of fear pressing him into the bed of congealed earth and mud – it was the blurred images of his father (for some reason it was usually the father), hunch-shouldered and stirring at something at the base of his allotment ground – that played hazily across his mind. And then – in a faint moment of distraction, as if downing tools for a passing cortege – his father would raise an eye from the soil and from the task in hand...gazing across a low wire fence, catching his son's eye...and for the briefest moment, there would be the trace of a smile, and then he would look away again and it would be as if he had always been looking away – distancing himself with the few hundred miles and decades of history that lay between them, leaving him, once more, to his private allotment matters.

The barrage of gunfire had begun to recede.

He eased himself up, sliding across the dirt in short bursts, like a lizard wary of encircling birds of prey – raising a cautious eye over the parapet.

There was little to see beyond shattered ravines of mud and a cold, heavy expanse of mist. No evidence of his oppos. No hints of movement, just a deathly hush like the dark side of some alien planet.

But he knew he needed to move.

He tried dragging his body along the wet furrows but nothing seemed to be happening: the period of stagnation and volley of warning voices echoing back and forth inside his head seeming to hold him firm. But he had to move. He pushed against the earth and dragged himself up the side of the crater, managing to part crawl and part slide his way along the final few feet of ground in front of him. And then – a renewed surge of panic – as he stopped, uncertain of the direction in which he should be heading.

He looked around, desperate to regain some sense of his bearings from the direction of artillery fire but all that lay before him was a sea of earth piles and shattered shell-holes. He looked left, right and then back again, knowing that, having finally regained his mobility, he must keep moving.

Raising himself slightly on his hands and knees, he found himself able to make a series of animated crawls, until a sudden return of machine-gun fire exploded above, around and seemingly below him, leaving him with little option but to drop once again, chest down in a nearby furrow of water and mud...and wait.

It was a further hour before any lull in the gunfire and for a while he lay, aware only of a distant thunder of exchanges somewhere over to his right.

He crawled a few feet and then resumed his crouching position, maintaining a slow but rhythmic movement coordinated by elbows and knees in what he hoped was the right direction. But even then he was aware of a renewal of barrages from somewhere behind him, reminding him that he must keep going – aware too that, at any moment, he might be called upon to lie in the mud and water and feign death.

He stopped to draw breath and spit grains of soil and slithers of mud from his lips. It was on re-checking his 'essentials', that he suddenly realised he had lost his revolver; it must be lying in the mud somewhere behind him. Returning to try to retrieve it was out of the question; the thickening mist already having reduced vision to a matter of feet rather than yards.

It was as he was crawling his way over the next 'heap' that he suddenly found his feet slipping and then floundering, and finally pummelling violently in the air, as his whole body slid and then ricocheted and then tumbled into a hole – a huge hole – almost a crater, in comparison to any of the other shell-holes that he'd had to negotiate.

And as he came to a sudden standstill, he turned instinctively, glancing from corner to corner, finally focusing on some movement in the midst of the far wall, and seconds later, finding himself gazing into the eyes of another soldier – a German soldier, his eyes wide and gaping back at him as if he too was in the grip of some hallucinatory trance.

For a moment neither of them moved, their eyes locked, their bodies frozen. Then, with adrenalin suddenly pumping him into the need for action, he made a grab for his knife, finding himself fumbling with his uniform and within seconds, the German had crawled his way over and was now above him, attempting to reach down too, their bodies locked in a kind of farcical embrace, until, unable to muster any real advantage, the German slid back and eased himself painfully a few feet in the mud.

Dingle leant back himself – watching – his hand still hovering round the belt of his uniform in expectation of the soldier's movements. For a few agonising moments, that's how it remained – their eyes locked like two scavenging beasts finding themselves in each other's territory.

It was the German who moved first, raising his arms a fraction and leaning back, extending the fingers on one hand.

'Tommy.....' he muttered, his voice hesitant and uneasy. His arm held at a forty degree angle in front of him.

Dingle said nothing but fixed his eye on the raised arm as wafts of shit mingled in the smells of earth and death drifting around the shell-hole. He shifted a fraction and leant back a little more forcefully against the mud.

The barrages of thunder and whine of shells had temporarily ceased, as if a mark of respect for their moment of 'togetherness'.

With time on his hands, Dingle lowered his eye to the man's face.

He was young; too young by far – a boy; maybe eighteen or nineteen – a few years younger than himself. His dishevelled tunic, caked in plaques of dirt laced in red streaks had twisted up his torso – contrasting starkly with a tiny pencil-thin tash – neat and almost ridiculous-looking on one so young, and midst a setting of mud-holes and death.

The German leant back, his head twisted to one side, and then maybe in a vein of some training-ground recollection, raised his right hand and held it, at first stiff and then in slight movements from the wrist. Dingle found himself aping his movements until his hand dropped and he resumed his pose laid back against the shell-hole wall, his head hanging lightly in the German's direction – noticing for the first time, the thick red blotch plastered across his tunic somewhere just below his left ribs. He was clearly injured – and likely badly – small scarlet rivulets had dried into the bottom part of his upper-tunic and laced the belt below. Dingle leant slightly for a further look. It could be a knife wound or maybe a bullet still nestling in there somewhere, biding its time. The German, following his gaze, turned his upper body slightly, as if to offer a better view, maybe sensing some hope of turning the injury to his advantage.

Dingle looked again. It looked bad – a congealed mess smothering most of the lower regions of his ribs thick and red, almost scarlet at its centre, panning out to darker, almost purple smears nearer the edge.

'Bullet?' Dingle nodded towards his tunic but made no move to get closer. 'Gun...?' He levelled a finger and cocked it a few times in his direction.

The German looked at him and shook his head, clenching his right fist at himself, moving it in short stabbing movements. Dingle dropped his gaze and eased himself back against the side, and for some moments that's how they remained – enemies – yet thrust together like escaped convicts skulking in a shell-hole of blown earth and mud.

Moments later a fresh barrage opened up and instinctively the pair thrust themselves into the dirt, a uniformed attempt to dig themselves in against the wave of shells.

It was some time before either mustered the courage to raise a head, their eyes meeting in a mutual moment of thanksgiving.

The German was making slight whimpering noises, his eyes tight and drawn against a new wave of pain from just beneath his stomach.

And then he was suddenly leaning down, gazing at his feet, a hand pressed to the wounded region of his lower side. Dingle watched him stare at the floor and then, bending low, wretch small pellets of pinky coloured phlegm just beyond him to his right, a soft mottled blancmange-like spew tipping out into the dirt, as the whine of another shell hit the trenches and disappeared somewhere over the distant lines.

There was little to be done. The pair hovered a moment, almost side by side, pressed against the flank of mud, catching their breath until finally, a ghostly silence seemed to have descended over the entire front.

The two turned to face each other, exchanging glances. It was with some relief that the German, his face drawn with pain, reached down and unclipped a pouch attached to the front of his belt.

Dingle watched – his hand hovering – his eyes suddenly flinching in renewed alertness, as the German withdrew a small picture and holding it firmly between first finger and thumb held it up, staring hard into the Englishman's face. It seemed to be a family, the faces indistinct and vague.

The German said nothing, but continued to push the picture in Dingle's direction, like a mother holding a photo of a missing son to the eyes of returning troops.

'Mein Familie,' said the German, his voice breaking to a series of hastily drawn breaths.

'Vater, Mutter....Bitte.' He stabbed the tattered print more urgently in front of Dingle's face, making attempts to draw attention to the two faces,

Dingle obliged but could barely make out their features. The German moved it a few inches closer, bidding him to take note, or even to take the photo from him.

But Dingle could only continue to stare. He could make out the long dark hair of a woman on the left and the spidery-looking features of a man on the right – presumably his father. He seemed to have a wide, bushy black moustache, which, if anything, looked a bit ridiculous on such a thin face.

Dingle nodded but quickly averted his gaze, his eye and ear focused only on hints of movement or approaching troops.

The German held the photo for a few moments longer and then replaced it and leant forward, returning his hand to the congealed mess at his side. He edged a little nearer to Dingle and looked towards him, almost forcing a half-smile, pointing repeatedly below his ribs.

'Trink kein bier,' he muttered, looking down at the twisted red fabric. He looked up again.

'Ich kann kein bier trinken.'

Dingle nodded though he wasn't entirely certain of the man's meaning; obviously to do with drinking beer – maybe saying he wouldn't be drinking much beer. His head had dropped, his eyes closing for a few seconds. He sighed and looked up again towards Dingle.

'I like beer,' Dingle said. 'In England....good beer.' He held his clenched fist and made pulling gestures towards him, indicating the process of drawing beer from a pump. The German looked up and nodded and smiled knowingly and then fell back, his hands clutching his side, a new wave of nausea seeming to overcome his distorted features.

Dingle watched the painful scene, and moments later, fumbled his fingers into a pocket, withdrawing a biscuit-bar which he held in the open and then nudged towards his lips.

The German managed to raise a head, and then – with a last gasp – made a sudden stabbing movement to his left, reaching to the lower part of his tunic, whilst looking back – wide-eyed and suddenly motionless – across the shell-hole. For that split second – he lay entirely exposed.

Within seconds, Dingle reacted – knife in hand, and – in as swift a move as he could muster – lunged it into the man's throat – the throat to stop him making any noise – and then watching as, after a brief writhing and choking, he fell back into the mud; his face silent and gaping, open mouthed – as if smiling – towards the skies.

Preparing to make his move, Dingle reached down the soldier's left hand side. Hidden there – next to the photograph – was a biscuit bar. He took it, placing it in his own pocket. And then quickly returned, taking the photograph, giving it a quick glance and placing it in a different pocket.

He eased himself up the lower half of the shell-hole, his eyes and ears alert to the possibilities of further machine-gun and rocket fire.

Keeping as flat as possible, he crawled out of the hole of mud, into the mud of the surrounding ravines.

[*A posthumous thanks to my late father, without whose help this story couldn't have been written.*]

Vigilance

As John Debbon unlocked the door and stepped inside the greenhouse, the familiar wave of warmth greeted him as did the row of tables neatly laden with pots containing small green shoots with varying degrees of tiny leaf growth.

He closed the door behind him and turned his attention to the utility table by the side of the glass front, which was covered in various sized stacks of brick-coloured plastic pots, an array of small metal tools and various packets, mostly about the size of packets of flour. A small tap next to the table dripped down into the drain surround. He'd have to do something about that dripping tap. Two lightweight coats hung on hooks on the other side of the door. He took one of the coats and pulled it round his shoulders and down onto his arms.

The second greenhouse stood about twenty feet away and his time was equally divided between the two. Beyond the greenhouses were several semi-cultivated squares of soil, many punctuated by lines of garden canes, connected in places by lines of string. When he wasn't busy in one of the greenhouses, he was busy in one of the squares, dealing with the shoots and other growths in various stages of cultivation. Beyond the greenhouses and the squares, a flat expanse of unkempt grassland stretched to fences with nothing much to attract the immediate eye beyond them. Small thickets of trees stood some hundred and fifty yards or so in the other direction and beyond them, more fields and hedgerows stretching out in the direction of Ongar.

Once he'd administered the water, he returned the watering can to its place and began his inspection of some of the plants.

Most were still tiny – fragile eyelashes striving for their claim to life in the incubated warmth of the greenhouse.

Wearing a tight white glove, reserved for the purpose, he laid his forefinger under the first stem, as frail as a baby's blood vessel, raising it gently, whilst another finger smoothed over the delicate surface of the leaf – about the size of a fingernail and the weight of a postage stamp. He leant down, looking closely at the green surface and taking a thin metal spatula, compressed the soil and compost mixture at its base. The process was repeated several times, and then several times again; each leaf receiving the same meticulous attention.

At one or two points he took a small magnifying glass from the pocket of his coat and flipped open the glass to enable a closer analysis. It took about an hour to complete the line, after which he went outside to begin work on the vines growing around one of the stretches of canes.

The owner of the nurseries, Mrs.Walker had known his mother from a time stretching back some thirty years or so. Her ageing had made working in the nurseries increasingly difficult and it was some time ago that she'd reluctantly had to retire from the active part of the business. Edna's son – John – who had lived at home with his mother, had been in her sights for some time: reliable, young and – as was soon to be proven – meticulous in his attention to detail. And, he had yet to be engaged in full-time work.

The 'deal' included a small bedsit flat, owned by Mrs. Walker and formerly rented out to various tenants, who'd come and gone over the years, leaving it currently vacant and available for occupancy. The flat was only seventy yards or so from the plot. Mrs. Walker had wanted Edna's son to move into the bedsit as part of the arrangement. He would then be close enough to keep a near enough constant eye on the nursery, which he had proceeded to do from the day he undertook his new-found employment.

From the onset he had learned fast and picked up the finer points of the trade quite admirably under the watchful eye of

Mrs Walker, who, particularly in the early days, guided him through the various processes and routines, ensuring that he received a thorough grounding in the business. As things had turned out, she'd soon been able to retire from direct involvement in the practice, secure in her mind that the allotments and greenhouses were in enthusiastic, and more than capable hands.

For her part she felt some responsibility for his well-being, having known his mother for so long and had kept a regular eye on his general welfare and disposition.

When she appeared in one of the greenhouses one morning, he was surprised to see her. She didn't often visit the nursery these days and putting his trowel to one side, he abandoned his potted plants for a moment to see what it was she wanted.

She confirmed that he'd worked exceptionally well and was doing a first-class job and the nurseries were a real credit to him. But she was going to ask him to do her a favour. She would understand if he preferred not to, because strictly speaking it didn't come under the terms of his employment, but she was going to ask him, partly because it would give him the opportunity to get away for a day; he was – after all – still young and it would be good for him to get a 'change of air' and see a little of the city.

The favour involved collecting a small parcel from an address in London. It could of course be posted, but she was a bit uneasy about using the post for such purchases, not least because it was such a burdensome business to arrange. She wondered if he would be prepared to go to London to collect the parcel for her. She would of course pay his fares and give him an extra bonus for his trouble, so he could perhaps enjoy a meal out and do a little sightseeing in the centre while he was there if he wished.

As it happened, he rarely gave a thought to life beyond the allotment, but he liked Mrs.Walker and could see that he would be doing her a big favour, so he agreed. She thanked him and promised he'd be given the full details nearer the day.

He nodded and returned to the business of relocating some plants into different pots and mixing a light compost for some shrubs behind the second greenhouse.

The day arrived for him to undertake the errand. He had met Mrs Walker at the allotment gate the previous day to get the details. She had greeted him with a cheery face and handed him an envelope containing the details of the address to collect the package and bus, train and Underground train details. She had then given him his fare and pushed two twenty pound notes into his hand – to cover expenses and a little 'extra'. He tried to tell her it was too much and wouldn't be necessary, but she wouldn't hear of it. He was doing her a favour and she wanted him to take advantage of a day-off from work.

The journey involved getting from the fringe of rural Essex into the centre of London. He would complete the journey partly by rail and then by catching the Underground. He had the envelope securely placed in his pocket along with the instructions regarding train connections. As he took his seat on the bus that would take him the first few miles of his journey, he cast his mind back to his youth when his mother had taken him for a day out to London. He couldn't remember it too well as he had been very young at the time, but he could remember it being an incredibly strange and busy place. She'd taken him to Buckingham Palace, The Tower Of London and they'd walked up Oxford Street hand in hand, him looking a little awestruck at the twinkling lights that seemed strangely entrancing on a cold wet December afternoon. But that was a long time ago, before his mother had died and he hadn't been back there since.

He was able to sit at a seat of his own on the bus, which was largely empty at this early stage of its journey through the peaceful setting of rural Essex. He had his book on 'Galvanised Hardwire Garden Borderings' in his shoulder bag, next to a cheese roll he'd made, should he get hungry later on in the day.

As the bus rolled its way into increasingly urban surroundings, he found himself drawn to the change in scenery: the endless shop fronts – neon illuminations of Fried Chicken and burger bars and quick-fix saver places and Asian greengrocers.

He checked once again with Mrs. Walkers' instructions and a few miles later, at the appropriate point, disembarked to cross the road to the station entrance to buy his ticket. It would be what they called a 'Travelcard' which enabled him to use both the main trains and the underground trains and buses, from here on. It was unfortunate that he hadn't been able to buy one before he started his journey, but there'd been nowhere out in Essex to buy one from.

The railway station was busy and he felt a little vulnerable amongst all these people and still a little unsure of the journey he was undertaking. He stood with his back to the wall, waiting for his train, having checked with Mrs. Walkers' instructions and the train-indicator board that he was on the right platform. He had the instructions in his coat pocket so there was no risk of losing them and could refer to them with easy access.

As he stood on the platform he kept half an eye on the people around him. In the summer there'd been some terrible bombings on an underground train in the centre of London and a lot of people had been killed. The Prime Minister had called on all travellers in the capital to be especially vigilant in the difficult days to come and, like any other traveller, he was determined to do his bit, as and when required.

The trouble was he wasn't sure what he had to do; look out for Asian men who could be carrying bombs in bags presumably. There were a number of Asian men dotted at various points of the platform and many of them were carrying holdalls. He would certainly keep an eye on them for any sign of untoward activity. At one point one of them reached inside his bag, but he was just getting his scarf because it was a bit chilly standing there on the platform. It was actually quite difficult to gauge which were likely to be suicide bombers – there being few obvious clues. One man was looking repeatedly up and down the line, as if in a state of some unease, but it could be he was simply eager to catch his train.

On the train and later on the Underground, it was even more difficult to be vigilant. Asians were everywhere! And not only did many of them have bags and holdalls, but they were pressed up against the door and each other and him, to the effect that it would be very difficult to intervene were any of them to reach into his holdall to activate his device. But....as it transpired, there were no bombers on this particular train and he arrived safely at the station Mrs. Walker had written down on the piece of paper.

He emerged from the grimy cream-tiled Underground station entrance rather like a child venturing into the street for the first time after a bombing in the Blitz. It was a frightening, unfamiliar world of whirring noises and frenetic activity. He reached for Mrs.Walker's instructions. He could see the name of the street she'd indicated, high up on the wall opposite, and as he gazed up towards the sky, the peculiar smelling air was already starting to have a prickling effect under his eyelids.

He checked once again with the notepaper and wandered uncertainly up the street, convinced that the gaunt grey buildings were closing in on him with every step. He found his eye drawn to their summits, where occasionally, a pale sun struggled through the gaps or rebounded off the panels of huge windows and large metal stanchions. As he walked he clutched tightly on Mrs. Walker's instructions – a spiritual light guiding him to the heart of his mission.

Despite the unfamiliarity of the surroundings, his task turned out to be a fairly straightforward business and it was soon clear that the address to which he was heading was not far away, about ten minutes in fact.

He stopped to look up at a large grey building and check the number with the number on the paper. This was definitely the place.

Once inside, business was swift and a few minutes later he returned to the street with a package wrapped in brown paper and held firmly under his right arm because it was too big to fit into his shoulder bag.

Back on the street he looked left and right and noticed a phone box about fifty yards up on the other side of the road.

The idea came suddenly. He would ring Mrs. Walker and tell her that he'd got into London safely and had already collected her parcel. He was sure she'd be pleased to hear the news.

He walked to the box and checked the phone number at the foot of the instructions. Only when he was about to lift the receiver to make his call did he realise there would be little point in venturing further; there was no receiver – just a few wires hanging loosely from the side of the metal box. And had there been a phone, there would have been no point in trying to use it as the slots to insert the money had been smeared with long-since hardened chewing gum. The kiosk was foul-smelling too, with a dark patch reaching from the corner to the centre of the floor. Above the phone box itself, he noticed a display of cards and stickers that covered most of the wall. Although scuffed at the edges and semi-obliterated with some strange words in black spray-paint, you could see that each had a girl's face or a drawing of a girl with a name – Carol, Sandy or Michelle with a phone number in bold print and words like 'waiting-for-you' and 'call now'. In some, there were two girls standing together, sort of face to face; '*something* - 'Babes' it said. And some were black girls and white girls together, with 'coffee-time' and 'coffee-and-cream' written alongside, though there was no café or address indicated. Maybe you had to phone up one of the numbers to get the details; but of course with no receiver and no slots to put the money in, there was no way of phoning anyone. He backed out onto the street and walked a little further.

He was feeling good and with something of a spring in his step, he headed off down the side road, not from whence he'd come, but in the opposite direction, where the road seemed

quieter and where there might be a seat or a bench for him to
sit and eat his cheese roll, though even here there were quite a
few people milling around, many of them females standing
around on the pavement as if waiting for someone to give
them a lift somewhere.

As he turned right into a street bordered by a row of shops
fronted with signs in words he didn't understand, he saw one
of the females standing against a wall some twenty yards or so
ahead of him. She was leaning back against the wall with one
leg cocked up and her foot pressed flat against the wall behind
her, causing her skirt, which was fairly short in the first place,
to rise a fair distance higher up her leg. She was gazing to the
ground as if lost in some private thoughts, but looked up as he
appeared in the periphery of her vision.

He looked at her briefly and then beyond her along the
length of the street for any sign of seats or benches, but there
didn't seem to be any in evidence. He would have to keep on
walking, but he didn't mind. The streets were quieter here and
he'd almost become accustomed to the strange odours that
seemed to waft and wave around his head with every small
shop or building he passed and he had Mrs. Walker's parcel
firmly placed under his arm.

The woman watched his approach and as he drew to
within a few feet, she said 'hi' in a light, playful voice. He
returned the greeting and stopped a minute to straighten the
strap of his shoulder bag which had buckled and was biting
slightly into his shoulder. Maybe she'd know where there was
a seat for him to eat his cheese roll.

'You alright?' she asked, speaking in a light, breezy voice, her
foot raised fractionally against the wall as she watched him
twiddling with the strap of his bag.

'Yes, okay,' he said, sliding his thumb under the shoulder strap
and along its length to check there were no more kinks to be
straightened. 'The strap's got a bit twisted that's all.' He looked
at her and then up the street for any turnings off to the left or
right, and then back at her.

She had a shiny dome of blonde hair that seemed to fit on her head like a pod and thick black mascara around her eyes. She seemed a friendly soul; the first person to talk to him since he'd left the underground train. She had a rather thin face, not unattractive, though so heavily disguised with lines of make-up it was rather difficult to tell. She wore a white blouse that was too tight and pushed her chest out in front or her in two quite prominent points. A small black hand-bag hung from her shoulder, her left arm draped casually across it. She looked at him and smiled again.

'You in a rush, or you got a minute?' she said.

He took a few steps forward and stopped. Her voice had sunk to the point that he needed to extend an ear in her direction. He looked up and down the road and turned his eyes to her.

'Don't know. I'm just looking for somewhere to sit for a while,' he said. 'I've been walking from the station and just need to rest my legs and eat my cheese roll.'

She lifted her handbag strap further onto her shoulder.

'You been shopping?' she asked, looking at the wrapped box under his arm.

'No, it's Mrs Walker's,' he said. 'I've just been to collect it for her.'

She continued to award him a quizzical eye, her foot still placed firmly against the wall.

'Whose Mrs. Walker then, your lady friend?' She raised a coquettish eye and smiled.

'No, she owns the nursery,' he said. 'She didn't want to come and get the parcel, so I offered to get it for her.'

Her eyes remained unmoved. He clearly wasn't one for striking up an immediate chord with strangers.

He was, in fact, giving very little away, except to divert his gaze to avoid direct eye contact that could be construed as 'staring' and a bit rude.

But finally he did look at her, almost smiling to himself. Things had been going so well, and she seemed a nice lady and had at least shown some interest in him and his parcel.

'So what is it?' she said, interested to get to the bottom of the mysterious box he held clutched in his arm.

'What?' he asked.

'The parcel. What's in it?'

'Don't know,' he said, looking down at it and securing it a little more firmly in the lock of his elbow.

'That's a bit strange. Carrying a box like that and not knowing what's inside it. Might be a bomb.' She laughed, her irises rising into the heavily mascara'd eyelids. He said nothing but looked past her in readiness to continue his journey down the street. She decided on a different tack.

'Look if you want to sit down and rest, why don't you come with me?' Her voice was suddenly softer, her head slightly tilted as if attempting to reason with a small child. 'I've got a little place near here. You can make yourself comfortable for a while, know what I mean? Eat your sandwich if you like.' She was watching him closely – looking for the faintest hint of a reaction. 'You got much money on you, here in the big city, all on your own?'

He told her about the forty pounds Mrs Walker had given him and that he had said it was too much, but she had insisted. She smiled and concurred something that he wasn't quite able to hear. She then raised her arm and still smiling, urged him to follow her, lowering her foot to the floor and making a move away from the wall of the building.

He stopped a moment – he needed to think. It was kind if her to offer and there were clearly no seats or benches in the immediate vicinity, but he was aware that in towns you can meet some strange people and you need to be wary about going off with them. Still, she was harmless enough, probably bored from standing around. At least he'd get to sit down, take the weight off his feet for a few minutes, eat his cheese roll and then he'd be on his way; maybe have a look around a bit or perhaps start back on his journey home. Where was the harm in it? He nodded and stepped after her watching the slight sway in her walk and clutching the brown paper parcel firmly in the crook of his elbow.

The stairs were quite narrow and she led the way to the top, turned left and opened a door, standing for a moment in the doorway for him to follow. It was a small room, quite sparsely furnished with faded thin-lined wall-paper which had drifted slightly from the wall in one corner. A single light bulb hung from a thin flex above the centre of a bed which was, if anything, a little too large in such limited space. At her invitation he took a seat on a small armchair and placed his shoulder bag and the parcel at his side. For a moment he sat, hands on his knees, his eyes passing over the simple contents of the room – the small cupboard, sink, chest of drawers and a small plant perched under the dark blue curtains, which were closed, casting that whole area of the room in semi-darkness. She brushed the surface of the duvet on the bed lightly and turned to face him.

'Would you like a coffee?' She clearly had every intention of him feeling as relaxed and comfortable as possible.

'No thanks, I don't like coffee.' He reached down into his bag and loosening the tie-up lace. She moved over to the sink and took hold of the kettle.

'Tea?' She held up a box to indicate it was there if he wanted.

'No thanks. I had a cup this morning before I came out,' he replied.

She moved to a sink next to the chest of drawers and held the kettle under the tap.

'Here we are together,' she said, speaking over her shoulder as she placed the kettle on a mat and flicked the switch. 'And I don't even know your name.'

'John,' he said, 'John Debbon.' He had placed the bag on his lap and now reached his hand into it to retrieve his cheese roll.

'Well hello John, I'm Suzy,' she said.

'Hello. Have you got a bin to put the cling-film in, or shall I just put it back in the bag?' he asked, looking round for a suitable receptacle.

'Don't worry, just leave it on the floor, I'll have to tidy up anyway later.'

He watched her as she perched herself on the corner of the bed. She looked at him and cocked her head slightly to one side again.

'So you say you've got forty pounds,' she said.

'Well I've got a bit more.' He reached for his wallet to confirm the fact. 'Mrs. Walker gave me money for the train too and I've got some left from that.'

'Good,' she said, raising a leg and crossing it slowly over the other. He took a bite out of the roll and cast his eyes over his surroundings.

'That your plant?' he asked, nodding toward the gloom by the window.

'No....don't know nothing about it,' she said,' It was just here in the room. Bit of a boring one really, hanging down like that. I like roses best – red ones.'

'It's a spider plant,' he said, taking another bite out of his roll.

'Spiders?'

'Spider *plant*. They're quite hardy but need watering regularly. The shoots can flower.'

'Thought you were on about spiders. I hate spiders.'

He took another bite, one hand cupped under his chin to avoid crumbs or bits of cheese spilling onto the chair or floor.

As he ate, Suzy leant back a little on the bed, the points of her chest poking a little more prominently through the straining white blouse. She stared at him for a moment, wondering how much longer she might have to lie there propping herself up on her elbows, but he was still busy eating his roll and avoiding dropping crumbs.

'Do you like me?' she asked suddenly, her left hand straying lightly over the upper part of her leg.

'You seem quite a nice lady,' he said, pushing the remains of his cheese roll into his mouth and rolling the clingfilm into a tiny ball before popping it into his shoulder bag. He hadn't realised how hungry he was, not having eaten since about half-past seven that morning.

Suzy continued to lie back, moving one leg slightly to the side. He looked at her and around the room until his eyes fell on the window sill. Having finished his roll, he rose and made his way over to the window. He looked down into the plant pot and instinctively placed his fingers under the thin slithers of leaves, most of which hung limply over his skin. He brushed around the base and gently pressed the area with his finger tips, but it was dry and hard, more dust than soil.

Lying flat on the bed now with one leg raised high and her short skirt hitched to only centimetres below her waist, she watched him.

'What you doing?' she asked, her head raised in puzzlement.

'The soil's too dry. It needs watering,' he said, stepping to his left to take a cup and hold it under the tap. He returned to the plant and gently tipped the cup, allowing the water to drip onto the surface of soil before gently manoeuvring it with his fingers and tweaking one or two dead bits from the side. She continued to watch him, intrigued by his concentration and the gentle movements of his arms and hands. She stood and walked over to a point just behind him, watching him knead gently at the base of the plant. She reached out her hand.

'Can I have a go?' Her other arm was resting gingerly against the arch of his back.

He removed his hands to allow her to reach into the pot and slide the limp strands gently between her fingers and press into the moistening soil underneath. He watched her for a moment and then laid a hand on her fingers, guiding them over the surface and pressing slightly.

'That's it, keep it gentle – use the tips of your fingers.'

She made tiny massaging movements in the soil, happy to follow his advice. He slid his fingers across the bones of her knuckles, guiding her to apply the appropriate pin-points of pressure.

'Just ease it gently round the bottom of the stem.....that's it.' She squeezed a little harder, pressing more firmly into the leaking scabs of earth.

She looked up, wondering if it was the moment for him to kiss her, but he had his eye on the thin strips of the plant's leaves, which were almost white and wasted with drought.

Only a few had the strength to maintain their line; the rest hung limply, like dead worms. He held them in his hands, levelling them under her eye.

'See how limp they are,' he said. 'They're virtually dead.'

She looked down at the thin lines lying across his palm.

'Mm...don't look much does it? D'you reckon it *is* dead then?'

'Pretty much.'

She abandoned the kneading and pressing for a moment and toyed with the idea of sliding a hand over his shoulder. He turned to look at her.

'They need looking after,' he said, looking at the pot, 'or else they'll die.'

He looked down for a moment allowing the limp strands to slide from his hand and drop down to the base of the pot.

He turned to make his way back across the room, where he bent to pick his shoulder bag off the floor and check that he had his wallet and instructions.

Suzy was standing at the far end of the bed, watching him lift the bag onto his shoulder.

'You going?' she asked.

'Yes I'll be off now. Thanks for letting me sit down and eat my cheese roll.'

She looked at him, still offering the faintest of smiles.

'Forty pounds is very reasonable you know,' she said, 'It's enough at this time of day.'

'I know. That's what I told Mrs. Walker. I told her I wouldn't need that much.'

She watched him turn towards the door.

'Don't forget your parcel,' she said. 'And by the way, my name's not really Suzy, It's Norma.'

'Oh,' he said.

'Bye Norma.'

He opened and then closed the door, holding the parcel tightly in the crook of his arm, leaving her standing by the bed next to the plant.

* * * * *

Visiting Grandpa

The kids clambered into the back seat of the wagon. He eased himself tentatively into the passenger seat, whilst his sister positioned herself behind the wheel, checked her face in the mirror and reached for the ignition key.

'Right now....seatbelts on. Come on....'belt up and be safe'. Have we all been to the toilet? Jenny, what about you?...Have you been? I'm not stopping till grandpa's.'

She answered in the weary tone of children accustomed to the ritual preliminaries of car travel.

'And Helmut.....What about you?...Have you been?

He had.

'What about you dearie? Are you okay?'

He was fine.

The wagon eased out of the drive, did a short reverse and made its way to the top of the avenue past the line of neatly boxed homes and tiny lawns. The pale April sun made half-hearted attempts to be cheerful and the wind had dropped.

'Alright in the back?.....Helmut, check Jenny's seatbelt. We don't want her disappearing through the front window if you don't mind. Just make sure it's in properly.'

'It is...I did it', pleaded Jenny, irritated that her reliability was being questioned. She was nine now for goodness sake.

'Well we're just checking dear, don't worry. Do you know how many children are killed in car accidents every year?'

There was an awkward silence...

'Well....an awful lot. And often because the seatbelt isn't on properly in the first place....So we have to be careful.'

With safety secured, as far as was feasible, they began the trip to grandpa's. A stream of sunlight brought a cheerful air to proceedings and they talked about television and horses as the wagon purred its way along the country lanes.

Grandpa's flat was on the ground floor next to two identically designed flats, below two floors of identically designed flats. The front lawn comprised two rows of tiny flowers and a bush sculpted in the shape of a small light bulb. The wagon pulled up and the back doors flung open.
'Careful now.....Don't go charging in there. We don't want grandpa thinking he's being burgled and getting himself a heart attack, if you don't mind.'
She turned to her brother, her voice dropping a little in tone.
'What about you dearie? What do you want to do? We'll be about half an hour. You can come in if you want to, or would you rather pop off on your own for a while?' The words were under-breath utterances, not for general consumption. 'I'd do that if I were you. It can be bit hard work with grandpa.'
'Okay...I'll pop down the sea front and then see you back at the car.'
He eased his way off the seat and stepped into the sunlight. After a parting word he made his way across the road and began walking down the avenue opposite.

The whole area had been designed with silence in mind. Nothing moved. Nothing stirred. Large detached homes stood alone and distanced from the road, from each other and from any manifestation of life.

Beyond them, and beyond the frail line of land, stood the sea – equally still and silent, like a still-life painting sheen of grey; the only sound - the rhythmic splash of water lapping lazily on shingle.

On the far side of the road along a grey path next to the deserted promenade was a single wooden seat. He crossed the road and seated himself comfortably, stretching out after the confines of the car. The featureless promenade and empty pebbled beach stretched as far as he could see. He leant back and crossed his arms and closed his eyes, relaxing in the thin warmth of the sun.

He opened his eyes to find a small dog standing motionless in front of him. It was one of those long brown dogs with short legs and a long nose. He gazed down and for a few moments their eyes remained locked. Eventually, the dog relented, switching its gaze to the left, but only temporarily, before returning to him, allowing a few moments further contact before turning to the right. He followed its gaze but there was nothing much happening in that direction either, and within seconds they were back to facing each other, eyeball to eyeball – like a game – lateral thinking.

He'd never been one for plants, dogs or kids, but this seemed a pleasant enough creature, certainly nothing threatening about it. He tried a different tack.

'Hello. What's your name?' he asked.

Ignoring the question, the dog turned again to the left, looking along the path and at the distant stretches of shingle, looking back only when it felt the time was right. And for a while they were back to square one – stonewalling each other, eyes locked in silence.

He decided on a little experiment. He'd stand up and start to walk away to see what would happen. There was plenty of time before he needed to be back at the car.

He stood slowly – so as not to startle it, and then walked about six yards, stopping to look back down the path. The dog had followed his every step but made no effort to follow him. He felt a bit sorry that it hadn't. It would have hinted at a kind of a bond between them....like mates. He fancied the dog was looking a bit sad about it, so he returned to the bench. Again, it looked away, as if checking for signs of activity, or maybe to show hurt that he had made a play of abandoning him like that. But then it was back, returning the stare, eyeball-to-eyeball; for some moments that's how they remained, each as determined as the other not to be the one to break the spell.

But, as is the norm with dogs, it ended. Perhaps becoming restless, or maybe just bored, the dog shuffled to the leg of the bench, offered it the ritual sniff and cocked its leg; and then continued its way along the path. At a point about twenty or thirty feet away it stopped and looked back – before making its way to the kerb and then across the road to the grass verge on the other side.

He glanced at his watch – time was getting on. He'd get back soon. If he took his time walking back along the avenue, maybe taking a brief wander along the promenade first, he'd be back pretty much at the agreed time. It was actually quite warm sitting there directly in the sun, quite pleasant, even if it was only April.

He got up slowly and made his way across the road, pottering his way along the iron pole of the promenade, feeling a brisk wave of sea air in his face and then at a suitable point he turned on his heels and made his way back into the avenue. The dog was nowhere to be seen.

He made a point of walking slowly. There was little to be gained by getting back to the car too early. He didn't want to be standing around waiting. As it happened, his return pretty much coincided with their goodbyes to grandpa. Minutes later they were back in the wagon.

'So did you have a nice walk along the promenade?'

'Yes...not bad. It's quite warm in the sun.'

'Good....Okay now...Are we belted up in the back? Helmut just check Jenny again please – we don't want any accidents. And did we go to the toilet at grandpa's? We don't want any crossed legs now.'

Mumbled confirmation as they moved off.

The blocks of flats and detached houses eventually gave way to a terracing of small shops, builders' yards and an estate agents – their windows cold and blank. As they approached the first set of traffic lights, they slowed and came to a standstill.

He looked out, eyeing the grass verges and the empty pavement weaving its way to the next block of buildings, when his eye was caught by a dark shape at the front edge of a driveway, a small brown dog standing on the grass verge – a long dog with short legs and a long nose. He leant his face into the window to stare out at it. The dog stared back – and for some moments they continued that way – eyeball to eyeball, until the lights changed and the car, switching into gear, began to draw away. He strained his neck maintaining eye contact as long as possible, until it finally disappeared from sight behind them.

'What have you spotted?' asked his sister.

'Nothing,' he said, his eyes returning to the road ahead.